The
Forged Coupon

The Forged Coupon

LEO TOLSTOY

Translation and Introduction by
DAVID PATTERSON

W. W. NORTON & COMPANY
NEW YORK · LONDON

The text of this book is composed in Avanta, with
display type set in Centaur.
Composition by The Haddon Craftsmen, Inc.
Manufacturing by The Courier Companies.

First published as a Norton paperback 1986

Library of Congress Cataloging-in-Publication Data
Tolstoy, Leo, graf, 1828–1910.
    The forged coupon.
    Translation of: Fal'shivyì kupon.
    I. Title.
PG3366.F3   1985   891.73´3   84-4144

ISBN 0-393-30300-4

W. W. Norton & Company, Inc., 500 Fifth Avenue, New York, N.Y. 10110
W. W. Norton & Company Ltd., 10 Coptic Street, London WC1A 1PU

    4 5 6 7 8 9 0

INTRODUCTION

*J*N HIS *Confession* (1879–1882) Leo Tolstoy was critical of the Russian Orthodox church, and as the years passed he became increasingly outspoken in his remarks against the church. As early as 1886 Pobedonostsev, the tsar's representative to the Holy Synod, recommended Tolstoy's excommunication, and on 24 February 1901 he got his wish. The attacks contained in *Resurrection* (1899), Tolstoy's last great novel, unraveled the last shreds of the church's patience, but Tolstoy received the news that he had been declared excommunicate with subdued delight. As a result of the church's action against the aging author, his popularity and influence soared to even greater heights.

By 1896 Tolstoy's followers were being imprisoned for possessing and reading his banned books. Indeed, he believed that the only honorable place of residence for a Christian in Russia was prison, yet much to his genuine dismay, the tsar refused to add the jewel of martyrdom to his crown of glory. Tolstoy did, however, receive many threats against his life. The mounting of religious persecution led him to write "An Appeal to the Clergy" in 1902, one of the most heated indictments of the church and organized religion ever produced; it was published in England in 1903. Other major works generated during these years include *Master and Man* (1895), *Father Sergius* (1896), and *Hadji Murat* (1904). It was throughout this period that Tolstoy worked most vigorously on *The Forged Coupon*, which was completed in 1904 and first published in 1911.

5

In *The Forged Coupon* Tolstoy assails a variety of figures representing a variety of evils, but his principal point is simple yet important: all people are brothers and the one thing needful in life is to love more. Two characters who discover this truth are Chuev and Stepan, both of whom ultimately personify Tolstoyan values —and both of whom go to prison, Stepan for murder and Chuev for his departure from orthodoxy. The real incarnation of all that is good, however, is Mariya Semenovna, a character who was probably modeled after Tolstoy's friend and disciple Marya Alexandrovna Schmidt. Tolstoy's daughter Alexandra described her as his one true follower, a woman who "was simply devoid of all pretense" and whose capacity for love was boundless.*

Because he was a man who fought evil in the world, it is not surprising to find that Tolstoy devoted this, his last short novel, to the theme of evil and redemption from evil. Although the evils of Tolstoy's world were large indeed, in *The Forged Coupon* we see that great evils can grow from very small seeds. Here Tolstoy would have us note that our most trivial actions can have the most profound consequences, for good or for ill: a father's cruel word to his child can end in the murder of a man, while a look of kindness can lead to the salvation of a soul. One need not ponder this for long to realize how deep a person's responsibility may run. Not only each of our lives but each of our deeds may have an impact far greater than we imagine. For a single pebble tossed into the ocean changes the level of the sea.

It will be said, and rightly so, that Leo Tolstoy was something more than a pebble tossed into the sea of humanity. It should also be pointed out that of all the evils he struggled against, the greatest he had to overcome were rooted in his own soul. In an effort

*Alexandra Tolstoy, *Tolstoy: A Life of My Father*, tr. by Elizabeth Reynolds Hapgood (New York: Harper and Brothers, 1953), pp. 389–90.

to free himself once and for all, he left his home at Yasnaya Polyana in the early-morning hours of 28 October 1910. Later that day he wrote, "It seems to me that I have saved myself—not Leo Nikolaevich, but something of which there is still a bit left in me."* He had planned to go to the Caucasus and take up the life of a peasant, but his flight was cut short. He fell ill along the way and had to stop at a stationmaster's house in Astapovo. His last days were spent in intermittent states of delirium, and little sense could be made of his ramblings. At one point Alexandra, who was with her father to the end, made out the words "to seek, always to seek." His last intelligible utterance was "truth . . . I love much . . ." On the morning of 7 November 1910 at approximately 6:00 A.M. Leo Tolstoy died at the age of eighty-two.

*Quoted in Ernest J. Simmons, *Leo Tolstoy* (Boston: Little, Brown and Co., 1946), p. 760.

Part One

I

*F*EDOR MIKHAILOVICH SMOKOVNIKOV, chairman of the Bureau of Fiscal Affairs, was a man who took pride in his incorruptible honesty and who was dismally liberal in his views; not only was he a freethinker, but he despised all forms of religion, looking upon them as nothing but the relics of superstition. He returned home from the Bureau one day in a very bad mood. The governor had written him a ridiculous letter from which it might have been supposed that Fedor Mikhailovich had done something dishonest. Fedor Mikhailovich was very much embittered by it and immediately wrote an impertinent and biting reply.

At home Fedor Mikhailovich felt that no one showed him an ounce of consideration.

It was five minutes till five. He thought dinner would be served right away, but it was not ready yet. With a slam of the door Fedor Mikhailovich went off to his room. Someone knocked at his door.

"Who the devil can that be?" he wondered, and then he shouted, "Well, who is it?"

Into the room came a fifth-year gymnasium* student, a boy of fifteen; it was Fedor Mikhailovich's son.

"What do you want?"

"Today is the first of the month."

"So? Is it money you want?"

The customary arrangement was that on the first of each month the father would give his son an allowance of three rubles

*The gymnasium is a secondary school designed to prepare students for the university.

for spending money. Fedor Mikhailovich frowned, took out his wallet, looked through it, and pulled out a coupon* for two and a half rubles. Then he took his change purse and counted out fifty kopecks more. His son said nothing and did not take it at first.

"Please, Papa, can you give me an advance?"

"What?"

"I wouldn't ask you, but I gave my word of honor; I made a promise. As an honorable man, I can't. . . . I need three more rubles, really I do. I wouldn't ask if I didn't need it . . . I wouldn't, but just this once . . . please, Papa."

"I have told you—"

"Yes, Papa, but it's only this one time."

"You'll get an allowance of three rubles and no more. When I was your age I didn't even get fifty kopecks."

"But all my friends are getting more than I do now. Petrov and Ivanitsky get fifty rubles."

"And I'm telling you that if you continue to behave like this, you'll turn into a swindler. That's all I have to say."

"Yes, that's all you have to say. You've never been in my position. I probably will turn out to be a cheat. For all you care."

"Get out of here, you good-for-nothing kid! Go on, get out!" Fedor Mikhailovich jumped up and lunged toward his son. "Get out of here! I'll have to whip you!"

His son became frightened and angry, but more angry than frightened, and with head bowed he started to march off quickly toward the door. Fedor Mikhailovich did not want to beat him, but he was pleased with his own anger, and for a good while longer he continued to shout abusive words as he led his son out of the room.

*In prerevolutionary Russia coupons clipped from interest-bearing documents were often used as money.

When the maid came and announced that dinner was ready, Fedor Mikhailovich got up.

"Finally," he said. "I'm not even sure I'm hungry now."

And with a scowl on his face he went to dinner.

At the table his wife tried to start a conversation with him, but he snapped back at her with such short, angry replies that she kept quiet. Their son also held his eyes on his plate and did not say a word. They ate in silence, and in silence they got up and went their separate ways.

After dinner the gymnasium student went back to his room, took the coupon and change from his pocket, and threw it on his desk; then he took off his uniform and put on a jacket. He picked up a worn Latin grammar text for a moment and then got up and locked his door. With a motion of his hand he swept the money off the desk and into a box, took some cigarette papers from the box, filled one with tobacco, rolled it up, and lit it.

He sat with his grammar text and notebooks for a couple of hours without understanding any of it; then he got up and, stomping his heels, began pacing about the room, recalling everything that had happened with his father. All of his father's harsh words and especially the evil look on his father's face came back to him, just as if he were listening to him and looking at him that very instant. "Good-for-nothing kid! I'll have to whip you!" The more he dwelled on it, the more angry he became with his father. He recalled how his father had said, "I see what will become of you —a swindler! Mark my words!"

"If that's how it is, then you probably will turn out to be a cheat," he thought to himself. "He doesn't care. He's forgotten what it's like to be young. So what crime did I commit? I simply went to the theater, had no money, and borrowed some from Petya Grushetsky. What's so terrible about that? Anyone else

13

would have sympathized, would have asked me about it, but all he did was abuse me and think about himself. Whenever he needs something, the whole house is in an uproar, but I, I'm a swindler. No, even if he is my father, I don't love him. I don't know whether it's right or not, but I don't love him."

The maid came to the door. She had a note for him.

"I was told to be sure to get a reply."

This is what the note said:

I have already asked you three times to pay back the six rubles you borrowed from me, but you keep dodging me. Honest men do not act in such a manner. I am asking you to send the money with this messenger immediately. I am in desperate need of it myself. Is it really possible that you cannot get it?

Depending on whether you return the money, I am your disdainful or respectful friend,

Grushetsky

"What do you think of that? What a swine! He can't wait. I'll try again."

Mitya went to his mother. She was his last hope. His mother was a kind woman and could not say no, so perhaps she would help him. But the little two-year-old Petya was sick that day, and she was upset about it. She got angry with Mitya for coming in and making noise and turned him down on the spot.

He muttered something under his breath and started out the door. She began to feel sorry for her son and called him back.

"I'll give it to you, Mitya," she said. "I don't have it now, but I'll get it tomorrow."

But Mitya continued to boil with anger toward his father.

"What good is it to me tomorrow, when I need it today? I'll just have to go to one of my friends."

He left, slamming the door.

"There's nothing else to do," he thought to himself, as he groped for the watch in his pocket. "He can tell me where I can pawn my watch."

Mitya got the coupon and the change, put on his coat, and went to Makhin.

II

Makhin was a gymnasium student who wore a moustache. He played cards, chased women, and always had money. He lived with his aunt. Mitya knew that Makhin was not a good fellow, but whenever he was with him, he involuntarily surrendered to him. Makhin was home and was getting ready to go to the theater: his dirty little room smelled like perfumed soap and eau de cologne.

"Brother, this is the worst solution you could have come up with," Makhin said after Mitya had told him the story of his misfortune, pointed to the coupon and fifty kopecks, and said that he needed nine rubles. "The watch could be pawned, but there might be a better way," Makhin remarked with a wink.

"What better way?"

"It's very simple," Makhin took the coupon. "Just put a one in front of the 2.50 and you'll have 12.50."

"Can that really be done?"

"Sure. Even with thousand-ruble notes. I've passed them myself."

"No!"

"Sure, why not?" said Makhin, as he took a pen and smoothed out the coupon with the fingers of his left hand.

"But this isn't right."

"Oh, rubbish."

"Just so," Mitya thought to himself, recalling again his father's abusive word: swindler. "I shall indeed be a swindler after all." He gazed into Makhin's face. Makhin looked at him with a calm smile.

"Well, what do you say?"

"Go ahead."

Makhin carefully traced the figure of a one.

"And now we'll go to a shop. There's one down at the corner; they sell photography equipment and such. I just happen to need a picture frame for this little number here."

He picked up a photograph of a wide-eyed young lady with very long hair and a gorgeous bust.

"Nice girl, eh?"

"Yes. Yes, very. . . ."

"That's all there is to it. Let's go."

Makhin got dressed, and they left together.

III

The little bell over the door at the entrance to the photography shop rang out. The students went in and looked around the empty shop with its shelves, equipment displays, and counters with glass cases. A plain-looking woman with a kind face came in from a rear door, stepped behind a counter, and asked what they needed.

"A pretty little picture frame, madame."

"In what price range?" asked the lady. The joints of her fingers swollen in her laced, fingerless gloves, her hands quickly and skillfully sorted out the various types of frames. "These start at fifty kopecks, while these are more expensive. Here's an attractive new style; it sells for around twenty rubles."

"Well, I'll take this one here. Can't you come down a little? I'll give you a ruble."

"We don't bargain here," the lady replied in a dignified manner.

"Oh, all right," said Makhin, laying the coupon on the glass countertop. "Give me that little frame and change, quickly. We'll be late for the theater."

"You have plenty of time," the lady replied; she started to examine the coupon with her nearsighted eyes.

"She'll look nice in this little frame, won't she?" said Makhin, turning to Mitya.

"Don't you have any other money?" the saleswoman asked.

"I'm sorry, but that's all I have. My father gave it to me; I'm supposed to get change for it."

"Are you sure you don't have twenty rubles?"

"I have fifty kopecks. What's the matter? Are you afraid we're trying to cheat you with forged money or something?"

"No, I didn't mean anything."

"Give it back, then. We'll go change it."

"How much do you need in change?"

"Oh, I think eleven or so will do."

The saleswoman clicked her tongue at that figure. She unlocked the desk drawer and took out ten rubles in paper money; then, sifting her hand through the change, she collected six twenty-kopeck and two five-kopeck coins.

"Would you be so kind as to wrap it?" Makhin asked, casually taking the money.

"Of course."

The saleswoman wrapped the frame and tied it with some twine.

Mitya did not start breathing again until the little bell at the shop entrance rang behind them and they were out on the street.

"Here are ten rubles for you, but give me the rest. I'll pay you back."

And Makhin went to the theater while Mitya went to Grushetsky and settled with him.

IV

An hour after the two students had left, the owner of the shop came home and began adding up the day's profits.

He saw the coupon, immediately noticed the forgery, and shouted at his wife, "Oh, you stupid, lame-brained woman! You imbecile! And why are you taking coupons?"

"I've seen you take twelve-ruble coupons yourself, Zhenya," the woman answered, confused, distressed, and about to cry. "I really don't know how they could have cheated me," she went on. "They were gymnasium students. He was such a handsome young man; he seemed so honest and proper."

"You're a proper fool," her husband continued to scold her, as he tallied up what was in the cash box. "I pick up the coupon, take a look at it, and see right away that someone has written on it. But it seems that you, in your old age, can look only at the students' faces."

The woman was not about to stand for this and became angry herself.

"That's just like a man! You sit and judge others, while you yourself throw away fifty-four rubles playing cards, and it's nothing!"

"It's different with me."

"I don't want to talk to you," said the woman. She went to her room and started to recall how her family had not wanted her to marry him, how they had considered his social position to be much lower than hers, and how she alone had insisted on the marriage; she remembered her little boy who died and how indifferent to the loss her husband was, as if it were a good thing that the little one had died. But as she thought about all this, she grew afraid of her feelings and began to hurry to get dressed and leave. By the time her husband returned to the apartment after having stepped out, she was gone. Without waiting for him, she had dressed and left by herself to go to a friend's place, a French teacher, who had invited them over for the evening earlier that day.

V

The French teacher, a Polish Russian, served his guests some fine tea with sweet pastries, and then they sat down at several tables to play vingt.*

The wife of the photographic supply merchant sat with the host, a military officer, and a deaf old woman who wore a wig; she was the widow of the owner of a music store, quite a gamester and an expert player. The cards went to the photography merchant's wife. Twice she set up a slam. Next to her was a small plate of grapes and pears; she was not at all in a cheerful mood.

"So Evgeny Mikhailovich isn't coming?" the hostess asked from another table. "We had assigned him a place as a fifth."

"He probably got wrapped up in doing the accounts," said Evgeny Mikhailovich's wife. "Today he's going over the figures for provisions, firewood."

*Vingt is a card game.

She recalled the scene with her husband and frowned; her hands, in their laced, fingerless gloves, began to tremble with anger at him.

"Well, speak of the devil," the host remarked, as he turned to see Evgeny Mikhailovich coming in. "What kept you?"

"Oh, this and that," Evgeny Mikhailovich answered in a cheerful voice, rubbing his hands together. And to his wife's surprise, he went up to her and said, "Guess what. I got rid of that coupon."

"Really?"

"Yes. I gave it to a peasant for firewood."

And with great indignation Evgeny Mikhailovich told everyone the story of how the unscrupulous students had cheated his wife; she interrupted now and then to fill in the details.

"Well, it doesn't matter now," he finished the story. When his turn came, he sat down at a table and shuffled the cards.

VI

Evgeny Mikhailovich did in fact pass the coupon off to a peasant named Ivan Mironov in exchange for firewood.

Ivan Mironov did business by purchasing a sazhen* of firewood at a woodyard, carrying it through the city, and dividing it up, so that for each sazhen he got five times the price he paid at the woodyard. On that day, which turned out to be an unhappy one for Ivan Mironov, he set out early in the morning with an eighth of a sazhen; he quickly sold that and loaded up another eighth, hoping to sell it too. He carried it around until evening,

*A sazhen is an old Russian unit of measure equal to about seven feet.

trying to get someone to buy it but with no success. He kept running into experienced townspeople who were familiar with the tricks played by peasants selling firewood, and they would not believe him when he assured them that he had brought the firewood from the country. He was getting very hungry and was frozen to the bone in his threadbare sheepskin jacket and his torn overcoat; toward evening it was twenty degrees below freezing. The old broken-down horse, for which he had no pity and which he was ready to sell for a pittance, had come to a dead halt. So Ivan Mironov was prepared to give away the firewood for a smile when he ran into Evgeny Mikhailovich, who was stopping by a tobacco shop on his way home.

"Please, sir, won't you take this at a bargain price? My poor old nag can't go another step."

"Where do you come from, anyway?"

"We're from the country. Our wood is good and dry."

"We know you. Well, what will you take?"

Ivan Mironov asked an exorbitant amount, then reduced it, and finally got the price he wanted.

"I'll cart it a little ways, but only for you, sir," he said.

Evgeny Mikhailovich did not haggle over the price very much because he was glad at the thought of passing the coupon. Somehow, pulling on the shaft of the cart himself, Ivan Mironov hauled the wood into the courtyard and unloaded it into the shed. The groundskeeper was not there. At first Ivan Mironov hesitated over taking the coupon, but Evgeny Mikhailovich was so convincing and seemed to be such an important gentleman that he agreed to accept it.

As he entered the maid's room from the back porch, Ivan Mironov crossed himself and thawed the icicles from his beard; next he tucked up the skirt of his caftan and pulled out a leather purse, from which he retrieved eight rubles and fifty kopecks in change for the coupon. Then he wrapped the coupon in a bill and put it in his purse.

After offering the gentleman a customary "thank you," Ivan Mironov was ready to race his empty cart to a tavern; he used not just the whip but the handle of the whip on the feeble old horse, now utterly exhausted and doomed to death, but the animal scarcely moved its legs.

In the tavern Ivan Mironov ordered himself eight kopecks' worth of wine and tea. He warmed himself up and even dried himself out, and in a most cheerful mood, he struck up a conversation with the groundskeeper, who was sitting at the table with him. He had quite a talk with the man, telling him all the details of his life. He related that he was from the country, from the Vasil'evskoe area, twenty versts* outside of town; that he was separated from his father and brothers and was now living with his wife and two children; and that the older of his children had just started going to school, but as yet it did not seem to do him any good. He said that he had a room there and that tomorrow he would go to the cavalry post to sell his old nag and see if he could buy a horse, assuming he could find one he liked. He explained that he now had about twenty-five rubles and that half of that was in a coupon.

He got the coupon and showed it to the groundskeeper. The groundkeeper was illiterate but said that he had exchanged such money for tenants. He said that the money was good, but sometimes one comes across counterfeit; so he suggested that Ivan Mironov change it there at the bar, just to be sure. Ivan Mironov gave it to the waiter and asked him to bring change; the waiter,

*One verst is approximately two-thirds of a mile, or just over a kilometer.

however, did not bring change but brought the bald-headed, shiny-faced bartender, who gripped the coupon in his chubby hand.

"Your money is no good," he said, pointing to the coupon but without giving it back.

"It's good money; a gentleman gave it to me."

"It isn't any good, I tell you; it's counterfeit."

"If it's counterfeit, then give it here."

"No, friend. Your kind has to be taught a lesson. You and swindlers like you are nothing but counterfeiters."

"Give me the money; what right do you have?"

"Sidor, get the police!" he turned to the waiter.

Ivan Mironov was drunk. Not only was he drunk, he was nervous. He seized the bartender from behind and cried, "Give it back! I'll go to the gentleman! I know where he is!"

The bartender jerked away and tore his shirt.

"Why, you . . . grab him!"

The waiter grabbed Ivan Mironov, and at that moment the policeman showed up. After listening to the whole story like a commander-in-chief, he immediately came to a decision.

"To the police station."

The policeman put the coupon in his own wallet and took Ivan Mironov, along with the horse, to the station.

VII

Ivan Mironov spent the night in jail with drunks and thieves. It was around noon the next day when he was summoned to the police chief. The police chief questioned him and then sent him with an officer to the merchant who ran the photography shop. Ivan Mironov remembered the street and the building.

The policeman called out the gentleman; Ivan Mironov was certain that he was the one who had given him the coupon. When the officer confronted him with Ivan Mironov and the coupon, Evgeny Mikhailovich reacted first with a surprised and then with a stern look on his face.

"You seem to have taken leave of your senses. I've never seen this man before."

"Sir, the wages of sin are death," said Ivan Mironov.

"What's the matter with him?" Evgeny Mikhailovich replied. "I'll bet you've just slept one off. You sold the wood to someone else. Wait here, though; I'll go ask my wife if she bought any firewood yesterday."

Evgeny Mikhailovich went off and immediately called the groundskeeper, a short, cheerful fellow named Vasily; he was a handsome character, unusually strong and clever. Evgeny Mikhailovich told him that if he should be asked where the last load of firewood came from, he was to say that he bought it at the woodyard, and not from a peasant.

"You see, this peasant swears that I gave him a forged coupon. He doesn't know what he's talking about; God knows what he has said. But you're an intelligent man. So just say that we buy our firewood only at the woodyard. By the way, I've been wanting to slip this into your jacket for a long time," Evgeny Mikhailovich added, as he gave the groundskeeper a five-ruble note.

Vasily took the money and flashed his eyes first at the bill, then at Evgeny Mikhailovich; he gave his hair a shake and smiled slightly.

"Everyone knows the common people are a bunch of mutton-heads. Lack of education. Don't worry. I know just what to say."

No matter how much Ivan Mironov begged Evgeny Mikhailovich to admit that the coupon was his, no matter how tearfully he implored the groundskeeper to confirm it, neither of them would budge: they never bought firewood off of carts. And the policeman took Ivan Mironov back to the station, now accused of forging the coupon.

It was only after a drunken clerk in the cell with him had advised Ivan Mironov to slip the police chief five rubles that he managed to get past the guard, but without the coupon. He now had seven rubles instead of the twenty-five that were in his pocket the day before. Of those seven rubles Ivan Mironov squandered three on drink; with a haggard look he went home dead drunk to his wife.

His wife was worn out from being sick and pregnant. She began to rail at her husband; he pushed her away, and she started to beat him. Without responding, he lay belly-down on the plank bed and broke out in heavy sobs.

It was not until the next morning that his wife found out what was the matter. She believed her husband's story, and for a long time she cursed the thief of a gentleman who had cheated her Ivan. Once he was sober, Ivan remembered what the worker with whom he had been drinking the previous night suggested: he decided to take his complaint to an attorney.

VIII

The lawyer took the case not so much for the money he could make as for the reason that he believed Ivan and was revolted by the way the peasant had been so outrageously swindled.

Both sides appeared in court, and the groundkeeper Vasily was a witness. The same story was repeated in the courtroom. Ivan

Mironov swore to God, swore on his own grave. Evgeny Mikhailovich could not change his testimony now and continued to deny everything with an outward look of calmness, even though he was tormented by the knowledge of the vileness and the danger of what he was doing.

The groundskeeper Vasily received ten more rubles and with a placid smile affirmed that he had never seen Ivan Mironov. And although he was trembling on the inside, when he was placed under oath he was calm on the outside as he repeated the words like a little old priest who had been summoned, swearing on the Cross and the Holy Gospel that everything he was about to say was the truth, the whole truth, and nothing but the truth.

At the end of the proceedings the judge denied Ivan Mironov's suit and ruled that he had to pay five rubles in court costs, which Evgeny Mikhailovich magnanimously remitted for him. As he was releasing Ivan Mironov, the judge instructed him to be more careful when bringing charges against respectable people in the future; he added that Ivan should be thankful that the court costs had been paid for him and that he was not being prosecuted for slander, for which he could spend some three months in prison.

"We humbly thank you," said Ivan Mironov, and he left the court shaking his head and heaving a sigh.

All this seemed to have ended well for Evgeny Mikhailovich and the groundskeeper Vasily. But it only seemed that way. What happened was something that no one could see, yet it was something much more important than what people see.

It had been three years since Vasily left the country to live in the city. With the passing of each year he sent his father less and less; and since he had no use for his wife, he did not send for her. Here in the city he had as many wives as he wanted, and they were not like the shrew he left behind. With the passing of each year

Vasily forgot more and more about the laws of the country and became more and more comfortable with the ways of the city. There everything had been dull, crude, impoverished, and confused, while here everything was good, refined, clean, rich, and orderly. He had become more and more convinced that people in the country lived in ignorance, like wild animals in the forest, while the real people lived here. He read the books and novels of fine writers and went to performances at the People's Palace. The simple folk in the country never even dreamed of such things. In the country the old ones said, "Live with a wife according to the law; work, so that you may eat; do not be pretentious." But here people were intelligent and educated, which meant that they knew the true laws and that they enjoyed their lives. And all was well.

Until the episode with the coupon, Vasily still did not believe that these gentlemen had no law at all concerning how one ought to live. It still seemed to him that even though he did not know their law, some such law nonetheless existed. But this last affair with the coupon—and especially the fact that, despite his fear, his false testimony resulted in nothing bad but rather brought him ten rubles—now convinced him that there are no laws and that one should live as one pleases. Thus he had lived, and thus he continued to live. At first the only money he had came from purchases made by the tenants, but this was not enough to cover all his expenses. So whenever possible he began to take money and valuables from the tenants' apartments, and he stole from Evgeny Mikhailovich. Evgeny Mikhailovich caught him; he did not take him to court, however, but simply dismissed him.

Vasily did not want to go home and remained in Moscow with a girlfriend. He began looking for a job and found a low-paying position as a groundskeeper for a shop owner. Vasily started work, but a month later he was caught stealing bags. His boss did not register a complaint, but beat Vasily and then fired him. After this incident he could not find a job; he spent all his money and went through his clothes, until he ended up with only a torn coat, a pair of trousers, and some worn-out shoes. His girlfriend left him. But Vasily did not lose his cheerful, good-natured disposition, and when spring came, he set out for home on foot.

IX

Petr Nikolaevich Sventitsky, a short, heavy-set man with dark glasses (his eyes hurt him, and he was threatened with total blindness), rose before daylight, according to his habit. After having a cup of tea, he put on his hooded sheepskin coat trimmed with lambskin and went for a walk on his estate.

Petr Nikolaevich had been a customs official and in that capacity had made eighteen thousand rubles. About twelve years earlier he retired, not entirely of his own free will, and bought a small piece of property from a young landowner who had squandered his money. Petr Nikolaich was married when he was still in the customs service. His wife was a poor orphan from an old line of nobility, a large, plump, beautiful woman who had given him no children. Petr Nikolaich was a thorough and persistent man in all his affairs. There was nothing he did not know about running a farm (he was the son of a Polish landowner); he was so knowledgeable about farm economy that after some ten years the run-down estate of three hundred desyatinas* had become a model farm.

All the buildings he owned, from the house to the barn and even the awning over the chimney, were sturdy and solid; they

*One desyatina is equal to 2.7 acres, giving Petr Nikolaich 810 acres.

were covered with iron and received a periodic coat of paint. In the shed where he kept his tools and implements, the carts, wooden plows, iron plows, and harrows were all arranged in order. The harness was streaked with dirt. The horses were not large, and almost all of them matched their farm: they were gray in color, well fed, and strong, each and every one. The thresher was operated in a covered threshing barn, the fodder was gathered into a special shed, and the dung wash flowed into a paved pit. The cows were also in keeping with the farm: they were not large, but they produced milk. The pigs were English. There was a chicken yard with a particularly hardy breed of hens. The trees in the orchard were neatly planted in rows and were covered with fruit. Everything all around was practical, sturdy, clean, and well maintained.

Petr Nikolaich took pleasure in his estate and pride in the fact that he had achieved it all without oppressing the peasants; on the contrary, he had won it by being extremely fair to them. Even in the presence of the nobility he held a moderate point of view, more liberal than conservative, and always defended the people whenever he was around landlords who advocated serfdom. If you are good to them, then they will be good. True, he did not overlook the mistakes and blunders made by the workers; sometimes he even pushed them around a little and was very demanding when it came to work. But the food and lodgings he offered were the very best; salaries were always paid on time, and on holidays he brought in vodka.

Walking carefully over the melting snow (this was in February), Petr Nikolaich made his way past the workers' stables toward the house where the workers lived. It was still dark, and the fog made it even darker; but a light could be seen in the windows of the workers' quarters. They were getting up. He intended to hurry them along; according to the order of the day, they had to take a team of six horses out to get the last of the firewood in the grove.

"What's this?" he thought to himself, as he caught sight of an open door in the stables.

"Hey, who's there?"

No one answered. Petr Nikolaich went into the stables.

"Hey, who's there?"

No answer. It was dark. The manure under his feet was soft and pungent. To the right of the door was a stall for a pair of young gray horses. Petr Nikolaich put out his hand—emptiness. He felt with his foot. Were they lying down? His foot felt nothing. "Where could they have been taken?" he thought to himself. Hitched up? No, they were not hitched up; the sledge was still outside. Petr Nikolaich went out the door and shouted loudly, "Hey, Stepan!"

Stepan was a senior worker. He came out of the workers' quarters at once.

"Yaow!" Stepan gave a good-natured cry. "Is that you, Petr Nikolaich? The fellows are coming right away."

"What are the stables doing unlocked?"

"The stables? I have no idea. Hey, Proshka, bring me a lantern."

Proshka came running with a lantern. They went into the stables. Stepan realized right away what had happened.

"It's thieves, Petr Nikolaich. The lock is broken."

"Are you lying to me?"

"They've made off with them, the dirty robbers. Mashka is gone. So is Yastreb. No, wait: here's Yastreb. Pestry is gone. Krasavchik is gone."

Three horses were missing. Petr Nikolaich did not say a word.

He frowned and heaved a deep sigh.

"Oh, if only I could get my hands on them! Who was on guard?"

"Pet'ka. Pet'ka fell asleep."

Petr Nikolaich brought in the police; he contacted the chief of the district police and the head of the Zemstvo*; he sent out his own men. They did not find the horses.

"Vile people!" Petr Nikolaich shouted. "Look what they've done. Haven't I been good to them? You just wait. Thieves, all thieves. From now on I shall not be so good to you."

X

The three gray-coated horses, however, had found their places. One, Mashka, was sold to gypsies for eighteen rubles; another, Pestry, was traded to a peasant forty versts on down the road; Krasavchik was driven to the point of exhaustion and slaughtered. The hide was sold for three rubles. Ivan Mironov was the one behind it all. He had worked for Petr Nikolaich, knew his former employer's habits, and decided to get his money back. So he arranged the affair with the horses.

After his misfortune with the forged coupon, Ivan Mironov drank for a long time and would have squandered all he had on drink, if his wife had not hidden from him the harnesses, clothes, and everything else that could be sold for liquor. Throughout his drunkenness Ivan Mironov was thinking not only about those who had wronged him but about all gentlemen and masters who live

*The Zemstvo was the elective district council in rural prerevolutionary Russia.

solely on what they can steal from their fellowman.

On one occasion Ivan Mironov was drinking with some peasants from Podol'sk. In the course of their drinking the intoxicated peasants told him how they had taken some horses from a peasant. Ivan Mironov began to curse the horse thieves for wronging the peasant.

"It's a sin," he said, "to take a peasant's horse. He's like a brother, and you cheat him. If you're going to steal, then steal from the gentlemen. They deserve it, the dogs."

From there the conversation ran deeper and wider, and the peasants from Podol'sk said that taking horses from gentlemen required cunning. You have to know their habits, and for that you need an inside man. Then Ivan Mironov thought of Sventitsky, the gentleman with whom he had lived as a farmhand. He remembered that Sventitsky was once a ruble and a half short when he paid him for fixing a broken axle bolt, and he remembered the gray-coated horses he worked with.

Ivan Mironov went to see Sventitsky under the pretense of applying for work, but it was only in order to look things over and find out what he could. Once he saw that there was no guard and that the horses were kept in open stalls in the stables, he brought in the thieves and pulled off the whole affair.

After dividing up the money from the horses with the Podol'sk peasants, Ivan Mironov went home with five rubles. There was nothing for him to do at home; he had no horse. And from that time Ivan Mironov began to run around with horse thieves and gypsies.

XI

Petr Nikolaich Sventitsky did everything he could to find the thieves. The incident could not have happened without an inside man. And so he began to suspect his own men and made inquiries as to which of the workers did not spend that particular night at home. He discovered that Proshka Nikolaev was not at home all night. Proshka was a short young man who had just returned from military service; he was a handsome, clever fellow whom Petr Nikolaich used as a coachman whenever he went visiting.

The local police officer was one of Petr Nikolaich's friends; he also knew the district police inspector, the chief of police, the head of the Zemstvo, and the examining magistrate. All of these figureheads visited him at his estate and were acquainted with his tasty liqueurs and pickled mushrooms—white mushrooms, honey agarics, and pepper mushrooms. They all sympathized with him and tried to help him.

"Yes, but you're the one who defends the peasants," said the local police officer. "I spoke the truth when I said they are worse than animals. You can't do a thing with them without a whip and a stick. You've said as much yourself. This Proshka, is he the one who works as your coachman?"

"Yes, he's the one."

"Have him brought here."

They sent for Proshka and started to interrogate him.

"Where have you been?"

Proshka tossed his hair; his eyes flashed.

"At home."

"What do you mean 'at home?' All the workers have testified that you have not been at home."

"Have it any way you please."

"Indeed, the matter is not as I please. So where have you been?"

"At home."

"Very well, then. Sotsky, take him down to the station."

"As you please."

Proshka did not say where he had actually been because that night he had been with his girlfriend Parasha; he had promised not to give her away, and he kept his promise. There was no evidence, so they let Proshka go. But Petr Nikolaich was certain that it was all Proshka's doing, and he came to hate him.

On one occasion, after he had hired Proshka as a coachman, Petr Nikolaich sent him to get some feed for the horses. Proshka took money for two measures of oats to an inn, as he had always done. He spent money for one and a half measures on feed, and the money for the other half portion he spent on drink. Petr Nikolaich found out about it and took him to the justice of the peace. The justice of the peace sentenced Proshka to three months in jail.

Proshka was quite conceited. He considered himself better than other people and took pride in himself. Going to jail humiliated him. No longer could he be proud in front of people, and he immediately fell into a state of depression.

Proshka returned home from jail embittered not so much against Petr Nikolaich as against the whole world.

As everyone had said, after his release from jail, Proshka grew lazy at his work and started drinking. Soon he was caught stealing clothes from a townswoman and was again sent to jail.

The only thing Petr Nikolaich found out about the horses was that the hide of a gray gelding had turned up; he recognized it as the hide of Krasavchik. Now the failure to punish the thieves troubled Petr Nikolaich even more. Now he could not look upon the peasants without disdain; nor could he speak on their behalf, and he tried to oppress them wherever he could.

XII

Although Evgeny Mikhailovich had not given the coupon a thought since he passed it, his wife Mar'ya Vasil'evna could not forgive herself for succumbing to the temptation of fraud; nor could she forgive her husband for the cruel words he said to her; most of all, she could not forgive those juvenile delinquents who had so cleverly deceived her.

Ever since the day she was cheated, she grew disgusted with all gymnasium students. She once ran into Makhin, but she did not recognize him because as soon as he saw her, he made such an ugly face that it completely changed his looks. But when she actually bumped into Mitya Smokovnikov on the sidewalk and looked him in the face some two weeks after the incident, she recognized him immediately. She let him pass and then turned around and followed him. After following him to his apartment and determining whose son he was, she went to the gymnasium the next day and met the religion instructor Mikhail Vvedensky in the lobby. He asked what she wanted. She said she wanted to see the director.

"The director isn't here; he isn't feeling well today. Perhaps I can be of service or give him a message."

Mar'ya Vasil'evna decided to tell the religion instructor everything.

The religion instructor Vvedensky was a widower, an academic, and a very proud man. Just the previous year he met young Smokovnikov's father at a certain social gathering. The two of them had a discussion about faith, in which Smokovnikov crushed him on every point and made a laughing stock of him; after that Vvedensky decided to pay special attention to the man's son. He discovered in the boy the same indifference toward divine law that he had found in the unbelieving father; he began to persecute the lad and even failed him on an exam.

Once Mar'ya Vasil'evna had informed him of young Smokovnikov's behavior, Vvedensky could not help feeling a certain sense of pleasure, since this incident provided him with evidence for his beliefs about immoral people who are without the guidance of the church. He decided to take advantage of the situation, as he tried to convince himself, in order to demonstrate the danger which threatens all who deviate from the church; but deep down, what he had in mind was revenge on the proud and complacent atheist.

"Yes, it's very sad, very sad," said Father Mikhail Vvedensky, stroking the smooth sides of the cross he wore on his breast. "I'm so glad you brought the matter to me. As a servant of the church, I shall try not to leave the young man without direction, but I shall also try to mitigate his edification as much as possible."

Then Father Mikhail said to himself, "Yes, I shall act in a manner that befits my title." Completely forgetting the ill feelings between himself and the boy's father, he had only the welfare and the salvation of the youth in view—or so he thought.

When the class in divine law was held the next day, Father Mikhail told the pupils the whole episode of the forged coupon and said that a gymnasium student was responsible.

"This behavior is vile and shameful," he said, "but denying it is even worse. If, though I do not believe it, one of you has done this, it is better for you to confess than to try to hide it."

Father Mikhail was looking intensely at Mitya Smokovnikov the whole time he was saying this. Following the direction in which Father Mikhail was looking, the other students were also staring at Smokovnikov. Mitya turned red, broke out in a sweat, and finally started crying; he got up and ran out of the classroom.

Once she found out about this incident, Mitya's mother forced the whole truth from him and hurried off to the photography shop. She paid the twelve rubles and fifty kopecks to the woman who ran the shop and persuaded her not to reveal the student's name. She told her son to deny it all and not to admit anything to his father, no matter what.

And, indeed, when Fedor Mikhailovich found out what had happened in the gymnasium, he called his son, who denied everything. Then he went to the director, and after explaining the whole matter, said that the behavior of the religion instructor was reprehensible in the extreme and that he could not overlook such a thing. The director sent for the priest, and there was a heated discussion between him and Fedor Mikhailovich.

"A stupid woman wrongly accused my son and then herself renounced her own testimony, while you could find nothing better to do than to slander an honest, truthful boy."

"I did not slander him and will not allow you to speak to me in such a manner. You forget my holy order."

"I couldn't care less about your holy order."

"Your false ideas are known throughout the whole city," the religion instructor replied, his chin trembling so that it made his sparse little beard shake.

"Gentlemen, Father," the director tried to calm them down. But there was no calming them down.

"According to the duties of my holy order, I must look after religious and moral education."

37

"Enough of this pretense. I really don't know: is it possible for you to be so superstitious?"

"I consider it beneath my dignity to speak to a gentleman like yourself," answered Father Mikhail, offended by Smokovnikov's last words precisely because he knew they were true. He had run the whole course of a religious academic and therefore had long since ceased to believe in what he preached and professed; he believed only in forcing all people to believe the things which he himself was forced to believe.

Smokovnikov was irritated not so much at the behavior of the religion instructor as at finding that this was a fine example of the clerical influence which is beginning to become so pronounced among us; and he told everyone about the incident.

As for Father Vvedensky, when he saw the emergence of confirmed nihilism and atheism not only in the younger but in the older generation, he became more and more convinced of the necessity to fight against it. The more he condemned the skepticism of Smokovnikov and those like him, the more he was convinced of the firmness and stability of his own faith, and the less he felt the need to examine it or to bring it into agreement with his own life. As he saw it, his faith, which was acknowledged by everyone in the world around him, was the primary weapon in the battle against those who would deny it.

The thoughts which the encounter with Smokovnikov produced in him and the unpleasantness at the gymnasium which followed the encounter—namely, the reprimand and the criticism he received from his superiors—forced him to accept a solution which had beckoned him for a long time, ever since his wife died: to take up monasticism and pursue the very career chosen by several of his colleagues from academia. One of them was already a bishop, and another had become an archimandrite as the result of an opening in the diocese.

At the end of the school year Vvedensky left the gymnasium, took the monastic vows under the name of Misail, and soon obtained a position as rector of a seminary in a town along the Volga.

XIII

Meanwhile the groundskeeper Vasily was walking down a road headed south.

He would walk during the day, and at night a village policeman would show him to the customary lodgings. People everywhere gave him bread, and sometimes they invited him to their table for supper. In one village in the Orlovsky province, where he was spending the night, they told him that a merchant who had leased an orchard from a landowner was looking for trustworthy watchmen. Vasily was tired of begging and did not want to go home, so he went to the merchant-orchard grower and was hired as a watchman for five rubles a month.

Vasily found life in his little hut very pleasant, especially after the apples began to ripen and the watchmen started gathering huge bundles of fresh straw from under the threshing machine at their master's threshing floor. All day long they would lie on the fresh and fragrant straw next to piles of still more fragrant winter and spring apples; looking to be sure that children were not sneaking up on the apples, they whistled and sang songs. And Vasily was a master at singing songs. He had a good voice. Old peasant women and peasant girls came from the village for apples. Vasily joked with them and gave them more or fewer apples, depending on what caught his fancy, in exchange for some eggs or a few kopecks; then he would lie down again. The only time he moved from the spot was to go to breakfast, lunch, or dinner.

Vasily wore a rose-colored cotton shirt with holes in it and nothing on his feet, but he had a strong, healthy body, and when the pot of porridge was taken from the fire, he ate enough for three, so that the old watchman was simply amazed. Vasily did not sleep at night but just whistled, just called out, and like a cat, peered deep into the darkness. Once a bunch of children from the village came in to shake down some apples. Vasily sneaked up and pounced on them; they tried to fight him off, but he threw them right and left and took one of them to his hut to turn him over to the owner.

Vasily's first hut was in the remote part of the orchard, but when the apples came in, his second hut was only forty paces from the master's house. In this hut Vasily was happier still. All day long he watched the gentlemen and the young ladies play, go for drives, and take walks; in the evening and at night they played the piano and violin, sang, and danced. He saw how the young ladies sat with students in the windows and exchanged caresses; then some would go for a walk down the dark linden path, where there were only spots and patches of moonlight. He saw how servants ran around with food and drink and how they worked for the sole purpose of feeding, refreshing, and entertaining the ladies and gentlemen. Sometimes the young gentlemen would stop by to see him in his hut, and he would select the best apples, juicy and bright red, to give them. Here too the young ladies would bite into the apples, crunching them with their teeth and raving over how good they tasted; they would speak French—Vasily knew what it was—and get him to sing.

Vasily fell in love with this life and recalled his life in Moscow; it occurred to him more and more often that everything turns on money.

And Vasily began to wonder more and more what he could do

to lay his hands on as much money as possible and as soon as possible. He remembered how he had come by his profit before and decided that he must not do it that way, that he must not grab at whatever lies in temptation's path, as he had done then; rather, he must first think things through, investigate, and do it cleanly, so that no clues would be left behind.

The last winter apple was taken to the Feast of the Immaculate Conception. The owner made a good profit, paid Vasily and all the other watchmen, and thanked them.

Vasily got dressed to leave (the young master had presented him with a jacket and a cap as gifts), but he did not go home; the thought of that crude peasant life was extremely distasteful to him. Instead, he went back to the city with some drunken soldier boys who had worked with him as watchmen in the orchard. When he arrived in the city, he decided to break in and rob the shop that belonged to the gentleman he had lived with, the one who had beat him and sent him off without paying him. He knew all the entrances and where the money was kept; he got one of the soldiers to keep watch while he broke the window overlooking the courtyard, crawled in, and took all the money. The whole business was skillfully executed, and not a single clue was left behind. He made off with 370 rubles. Vasily gave a hundred rubles to his friend and took the rest to another city, where he caroused with friends and acquaintances.

XIV

In the meantime Ivan Mironov had become a clever, daring, and successful horse thief. His wife Afim'ya, who had previously scolded him for his wrongdoings, as she called them, was now content. She was proud of her husband because he wore a sheepskin coat, and she herself had a shawl and a fur coat.

Everyone in the village and surrounding areas knew that not a single horse theft was managed without him, but they were afraid to bring an accusation against him, and whenever he did fall under suspicion, he got off scot-free. His last horse theft was at a night watch in Kolotovka. Whenever he could, Ivan Mironov determined whom he could rob; above all he liked to steal from landowners and merchants. But it was more difficult to steal from landowners and merchants. And so whenever there were no suitable landowners and merchants, he stole from the peasants. Thus he rounded up what horses he could from the night watch in Kolotovka.

He did not carry out the affair himself but rather put a clever lad named Gerasim up to it. It was dawn before the peasants noticed that the horses were gone and set out to search along the roads. The horses, however, were in a ravine in a government forest. Ivan Mironov planned to keep them there until the next night and then take them forty versts away to a groundskeeper he knew. Ivan Mironov took Gerasim into the forest, brought him meat pies and vodka, and then went home by a wooded path, hoping he would not meet anyone along the way. Unfortunately, he ran into a military warden.

"Been out looking for mushrooms?" the soldier asked.

"Yes, but couldn't find any today," Ivan Mironov answered, pointing to a basket he carried for just such occasions.

"Well, this isn't a summer for mushrooms," said the soldier. "Might have to go without." And he passed on by.

The soldier knew that something was not quite right here. There was no reason for Ivan Mironov to be wandering about in the government forest so early in the morning. The soldier turned back and started rummaging around in the woods. Near the ravine he heard the sound of horses snorting and quietly went to the place where the sounds were coming from. The grass in the ravine was beaten down, and there were piles of horse manure. In the distance Gerasim was sitting and eating something, and two horses stood tied to a tree.

The soldier hurried off to the village and fetched the bailiff, the commissioner of police, and two witnesses. They approached the place where Gerasim was from three different directions and seized him. Gerasim did not try to deny anything and in his state of drunkenness immediately confessed everything. He told the story of how Ivan Mironov had given him liquor and had put him up to it and said that Ivan had promised to come to the forest for the horses later that day. The peasants left Gerasim and the horses in the forest and then took up hiding places to wait for Ivan Mironov. When it started to get dark, they heard a whistle. Gerasim answered. Just as Ivan Mironov started to come down from the hill, they jumped him and took him off to the village. The next morning a crowd gathered in front of the bailiff's office.

They brought Ivan Mironov out and began to interrogate him. Stepan Pelageyushkin, a tall, round-shouldered, long-armed peasant with an aquiline nose and a dark expression on his face, was the first to begin the questioning. Stepan was a solitary peasant who had served his time in the military. He left his father and had just begun to manage for himself, when a horse was stolen from him. After spending a year working in the mines, Stepan again bought two horses. Both of them were stolen.

"Tell me where my horses are," Stepan began, growing pale with rage, looking sternly, now at the ground, now into Ivan's face.

Ivan Mironov refused to answer. Stepan struck him in the face and hit him in the nose, from which blood began to flow.

"Speak, or I'll kill you!"

Ivan remained silent, his head hanging down. Stepan hit him with his big fist once, twice. Ivan was still silent and would only turn his head first to one side and then to the other.

"Everyone! Beat him!" the bailiff shouted.

And they all began to hit him. Ivan Mironov fell in silence and then cried, "Savages! Devils! Beat me to death! I'm not afraid of you!"

Then Stepan took a huge stone and hit Ivan Mironov over the head with it.

XV

Ivan Mironov's murderers were brought to trial. Stepan Pela-geyushkin was among the murderers. The charges against him were more severe than those against the others, since everyone testified that he hit Ivan Mironov over the head with a stone. At the trial Stepan made no attempt to hide anything, explaining that when the last pair of horses were stolen from him, he notified the police; he said that according to some gypsies, tracks could be found, yet the district police officer would not see him and did not undertake any kind of search.

"What are we to do with someone like that? He has ruined us."

"But why did you beat him, when the others did not?" the prosecutor asked.

"That isn't true. Everyone beat him. The whole village was bent on killing him. I just finished him off."

The judge was struck by Stepan's expression of utter calm as he told the story of what he had done, of how Ivan Mironov was beaten and how he had finished him off.

Stepan actually saw nothing terrible in this murder. In the service he had to shoot a soldier, and in that, as in the murder of Ivan Mironov, he saw nothing terrible. People kill people. Today him, tomorrow me.

Stepan was given a light sentence: one year in prison. They took his peasant clothes from him, sent him to a room in the armory, and dressed him in a convict's overalls and shoes.

Stepan never had any respect for authority, but now he was convinced that all authorities, all gentlemen, all except the tsar, who alone had compassion for the people and was just, were criminals who lived off the blood of the people. The stories told by the exiles and convicts with whom he went to prison confirmed such a view. One was sentenced to hard labor after the authorities had convicted him of robbery; another was sentenced for striking an official who started to confiscate the peasant's property for no reason; a third was convicted of counterfeiting. No matter what the gentlemen and the merchants did, they got away with it, while the peasants and the poor were sent to jail to feed the lice for the slightest infraction.

His wife visited him in jail. Without him it was going so badly for her that she went bankrupt and was completely ruined, and she and the children had begun to beg. His wife's poverty embittered Stepan even more. He became angry with everyone in the prison and once nearly took an axe to the cook because a year had been added to his sentence. During that year he found out that his wife had died and that he had lost his home. . . .

When Stepan had served his term, he was sent back to the armory. The clothes he had worn when he was sentenced were taken off a shelf and given back to him.

"So where do I go now?" he asked the quartermaster sergeant as he was getting dressed.

"Home, of course."

"I have no home. I'll probably have to go on the road. To rob people."

"And if you rob people, you'll be sent back to us."

"That's the way it has to be, I guess."

And Stepan left. He made his way toward his home in spite of everything. There was nowhere else to go.

Before he reached home, he stopped to spend the night at an inn he knew of which had a tavern with it.

The innkeeper was a heavy-set commoner from the city of Vladimir. He knew Stepan. And he knew that Stepan had met with the misfortune of being sent to jail. And he let Stepan stay the night with him.

This well-to-do commoner had stolen away the wife of a neighboring peasant and was living with her; she served as a housemaid and a wife to him.

Stepan knew all about this affair—how the innkeeper had wronged the peasant, how the vile wench had left her husband and had gotten fat on good food; she would sit down to tea all sweaty, and she treated Stepan to some tea out of charity. There were no other travelers at the inn. They let Stepan spend the night in the kitchen. Matrena put everything in order and then went to her room.

Stepan lay down on the stove, but he could not sleep and kept knocking against some wood that had been left there to dry. He could not stop thinking about the fat, potbellied innkeeper with his cotton shirt sticking out from under his belt, faded from having been washed over and over. He kept thinking about slitting that potbelly open with a knife and letting the bowels run out. The wench too. He would say to himself, "Oh, the devil take them; I'm leaving tomorrow." And then he would remember Ivan Mironov, and again he would start thinking about the potbellied innkeeper and Matrena's white, sweaty throat. Yes, kill them both alike.

A second cock crowed. Do it now; it will soon be dawn. He had noticed a knife the evening before, and an axe. He slipped off the stove, grabbed the knife and the axe, and went out of the kitchen. Just as he went out, he heard a latch click behind a door. The innkeeper came out. Stepan did not do what he had planned to do. He did not use the knife but took the axe and brought it down on the man's head. The innkeeper fell against the lintel and down to the floor.

Stepan went into Matrena's room. She jumped up and stood beside her bed wearing nothing but her nightgown. Stepan killed her with the same axe.

Then he lit a candle, took the money from the desk, and left.

XVI

In the district's main town, in a house that was isolated from all the other buildings, lived an old man, who was a former official and a drunkard, with his two daughters and a son-in-law. The married daughter also drank and led a wretched life. Her older sister, the widow Mariya Semenovna, was a skinny, wrinkled, fifty-year-old woman who supported the rest of them all by herself: she had a pension of 250 rubles. The whole family ate on this money. Mariya Semenovna was also the only one who did any work around the house. She took care of her weak, drunken old father and her sister's little boy; she prepared the meals and did the cleaning. And as it always happens, she was the one who had to handle whatever business that had to be taken care of. Yet all three of them abused her, and her brother-in-law even beat her whenever he was drunk. She endured it all quietly and humbly, and as it always happens, the more she had to do, the more successful she was at doing it. She even denied herself to help the poor; she gave away her clothes and helped to care for the sick.

The lame village tailor, a man with only one leg, once did some work for Mariya Semenovna. He altered a waistcoat for the old man and put a cloth lining in a sheepskin coat for Mariya Semenovna—so she could go to the market when winter came.

The lame tailor was an intelligent and observant man who had seen many different people in the course of his work; and because of his lameness, he always had to sit and was therefore always in a thinking position. After spending a week with Mariya Semenovna, he could not admire her life enough. On one occasion he was sewing in the kitchen when she came in to wash some towels; she struck up a conversation with him about his life, about how his brother had offended him and how the two of them had detached themselves from each other.

"I thought that one day things would be better for me, but I'm still poor."

"It is better not to change but to live as you live," said Mariya Semenovna.

"You know, Mariya Semenovna, you truly amaze me, the way you alone—indeed, completely alone—go to so much trouble for people. Yet I see little good in those people."

Mariya Semenovna did not say anything.

"I suppose you've gathered from books that the reward for that will come in the next world."

"We know nothing about that," said Mariya Semenovna. "Only that we should live as best we can."

"And is that to be found in books?"

"It is," she said, and she read to him the Sermon on the Mount

from the Gospel. The tailor thought it over. And when he settled
his account with her and went home, he was still thinking about
what he had seen in Mariya Semenovna and what she had said and
read to him.

XVII

Petr Nikolaich changed his attitude toward the people, and they
changed their attitude toward him. Not a year went by without
their cutting down twenty-seven oak trees and burning down an
uninsured threshing barn and threshing floor. Petr Nikolaich decided that he could no longer live among the local people.

At that same time the Liventsovs were looking for a manager
for their estate, and the head of the district recommended Petr
Nikolaich as the best one in the region. The Liventsov estate was
huge, but it was not producing any income; the peasants were
taking all the profits. Petr Nikolaich took on the job of putting
everything in order; he leased his property, and he and his wife
moved to the distant province of Povolzh'e.

Petr Nikolaich had always had a love for law and order, and
now he had even less tolerance for this wild, coarse people who,
wherever possible, illegally seized property that did not belong to
them. He was glad to have the opportunity to teach them a lesson,
and he attended to his business in a strict manner. He had one
peasant sent to jail for stealing lumber; another he beat unmerci-
fully with his own hands because the man did not turn off to the
side of the road and take off his hat. There was an argument about
the meadows, which the peasants regarded as their own, and Petr
Nikolaich proclaimed to them that if they allowed their livestock
to go into the meadows, he would have the animals confiscated.

Spring came, and as the year before, the peasants let their livestock out into the landlord's meadows. Petr Nikolaich gathered all the workers together and ordered them to drive the livestock into the landlord's corral. The peasant men were plowing their fields, and the workers rounded up the livestock despite the out-cries of the peasant women. When they returned from their work, the peasant men got together and went to the landlord's corral to demand their animals. Petr Nikolaich greeted them with a rifle on his shoulder (he had just returned from making his rounds) and declared to them that he would not return their livestock unless they paid fifty kopecks for each head of cattle and ten for each sheep. The peasants began to shout that the meadows were theirs, owned by them and their fathers and their grandfathers, and that Petr Nikolaich had no right to take away someone else's livestock.

"Give us our livestock and there will be no trouble," said one old man, stepping toward Petr Nikolaich.

"What trouble might there be?" Petr Nikolaich cried, com-pletely pale, as he moved toward the old man.

"Spare yourself from sin. You cheat."

"What?" Petr Nikolaich yelled and hit the old man in the face.

"You wouldn't dare fight us. Let's take the animals by force, men."

The crowd moved forward. Petr Nikolaich tried to leave, but they would not let him. He started to fight back. The rifle went off and killed one of the peasants. Suddenly there was a scuffle. They trampled Petr Nikolaich. And five minutes later his muti-lated body was dragged off to a ravine.

A military trial was held for the murderers, and two men were sentenced to be hanged.

XVIII

In the village where the tailor lived, five rich peasants leased 105 desyatinas of fertile, arable land that was black as tar for eleven hundred rubles and parceled it out to the peasants for fifteen to eighteen rubles apiece. Not a single plot brought in less than twenty rubles, so there was a good profit. Those who had leased the land took five desyatinas for themselves, and it did not cost them a thing. When one of their partners died, they invited the lame tailor to come in with them as a new partner.

At the time when they started dividing up the land, the tailor had stopped drinking vodka. And when the talk got around to how much land should be given to whom, the tailor said that they did not need to take too much from the tenants, but only as much as necessary.

"How's that?"

"It wouldn't be Christian to do otherwise. It may be very well for gentlemen, but we are peasants. We must act according to God's way. Such is the law of Christ."

"And where is this law?"

"In the book, in the Gospel. Come over Sunday; I'll read, and we'll have a talk."

Not all of them went to see the tailor on Sunday, but three did go, and he read to them.

He read five chapters of Matthew, and then they began to talk. They all listened, but Ivan Chuev was the only one who embraced it. And as he embraced it, he began to live according to the ways of God in all things. And so his family began to live. He refused to take any of the land that was left over, except his allotted share.

People began to call on Ivan and the tailor, and they began to understand and embrace the teachings; they gave up smoking, drinking, and swearing, and turned to helping one another. They quit going to church and returned their icons to the priest. There were seventeen such households, sixty-five souls in all. This frightened the priest, and he informed the bishop. The bishop considered what was to be done and decided to send Father Misail, the former religion instructor from the gymnasium, to the village.

XIX

The bishop sat down with Misail and discussed the news that had developed in his diocese.

"It's all the result of ignorance and spiritual weakness. You are a learned man. I'm depending on you. Go, summon the people, and explain to them."

"With my lord's blessing, I shall try," said Father Misail. He was glad to have this assignment. He was always glad to demonstrate what he believed wherever he could. And when he was converting others, he was convinced more strongly than ever of what he believed.

"Try hard. I have suffered a great deal over my flock," the bishop replied, leisurely extending his plump, white hand to take the cup of tea which the servant had just brought him.

"Is this all the jam? Bring some more," he turned to the servant. Then, continuing his speech, he said to Misail, "It is very, very painful to me."

Misail was glad to prove himself. But as he was a man of modest means, he asked for money to cover the costs of the trip; and fearful of opposition from the crude people, he also asked for an order from the governor stating that the local police were to help him if need be.

The bishop arranged everything for him. With the help of his servant and his cook, Misail gathered the food and provisions he needed to have in supply before going off to the middle of nowhere and left for his destination. As he set out on this mission, Misail experienced the pleasant feeling of being aware of the importance of his service and of putting an end to all the doubts he had about his faith; in fact, he was now completely certain of its truth.

His thoughts were not focused on the essence of faith—that was confessed according to axiom—but on the refutation of those objections which arose in connection with its outward forms.

XX

The village priest and his wife received Misail with all the honors, and on the day after his arrival they gathered the people together in the church. Dressed in a new silk cassock with a cross hanging on his breast and his hair neatly combed, Misail went up to the pulpit. The priest stood next to him, with the sextons and choirboys off in the background; policemen were stationed at the side doors. The sectarians arrived wearing dirty, wrinkled sheepskin coats.

After the opening prayer Misail gave the sermon, exhorting those who had strayed to return to the bosom of the Mother Church, threatening them with the tortures of hell, and promising forgiveness for all who would repent.

The sectarians remained silent. When they were questioned, they answered.

To the question of why they had broken away, they answered

that wooden and hand-made gods were held sacred in the church
and that not only was nothing of the sort found in the Scriptures,
but the prophets bore witness to the contrary. When Misail asked
Chuev whether it was true that they referred to the holy icons as
boards, Chuev replied, "All you have to do is examine any icon
you like, and you will see for yourself." When asked why they did
not acknowledge the priesthood, they replied that in the Scriptures it says, "Freely you have received, so freely give,"* and that
the priests bestow their blessings only for money. Ivan and the
tailor objected calmly but firmly to all of Misail's attempts to find
support in the Holy Scriptures, pointing to the Scriptures which
they themselves knew so well. Misail grew angry and threatened
them with secular authority. To this the sectarians said, "If they
have persecuted me, they will also persecute you."†

All this came to nothing, and everything would have gone well,
but the next day at mass Misail gave a sermon on the harmfulness
of those leading others astray, saying that they deserved every
manner of punishment. When the people left the church, they
began discussing how the atheists might be taught a lesson, so that
they would no longer disturb others.

That same day a scuffle broke out in the village, just when
Misail was snacking on some salmon and whitefish with the arch-
deacon and an inspector who had just arrived from the city. The
orthodox believers had crowded around Chuev's cottage and were
waiting for those inside to come out so they could beat them to
a pulp. There were twenty peasant men and women among the
sectarians. Misail's sermon and now the crowd of orthodox believers and their threatening words aroused in the sectarians feelings
of anger which they had never felt before. Evening was coming

*Words Jesus spoke in Matthew 10 : 8.
†Jesus said this to his disciples in John 15 : 20.

on, and it was time for the women to milk the cows. The orthodox believers were still waiting outside, and when a few people came out, they were attacked and driven back into the cottage. They discussed what to do but could not agree.

The tailor said they must not defend themselves but endure. Chuev, however, said that if they endured that way, they would all be slaughtered. He grabbed a poker and went out to the street. The orthodox believers fell upon him.

"So be it, according to the law of Moses!" he cried and started fighting back; he put out the eye of one of his attackers, and those who had stayed in the cottage darted out and returned home.

Chuev was tried for sedition and blasphemy and was sentenced to exile.

As for Father Misail, he was rewarded and made an archimandrite.

XXI

Two years earlier a beautiful, healthy girl, an Oriental type named Turchaninova, came to Petersburg from the Cossack territory along the Don River to study. This young woman met a student in Petersburg named Tyurin, the son of a Zemstvo official from the Simbirsk region, and fell in love with him. But she did not fall in love with him in the way that a woman usually falls in love, with the longing to become his wife and the mother of his children; rather, it was the love of one friend for another, nourished largely by a common indignation and hatred toward the existing establishment and the people who were its representatives. Their love was also fostered by an awareness of their intellectual, educational, and moral superiority over those representatives.

Turchaninova was a capable learner and easily memorized the lectures and passed the exams; not only that, she devoured huge quantities of the latest books. She was certain that her calling did not lie in bearing and rearing children; indeed, she looked upon such a prospect with loathing and disgust. No, her destiny lay in destroying the existing establishment, which had suppressed the greatest strengths of the people, and in showing the people the way to the new path in life that the latest European writers had opened up to her.

She was shapely, fair, and beautiful; her rosy complexion, flashing dark eyes, and long black braids excited in men feelings she did not welcome and could not share. Thus she occupied herself completely with her word-of-mouth propaganda campaign. Nonetheless, it pleased her that she aroused these feelings; although she did not dress in an alluring manner, she did not neglect her appearance. It pleased her that she was liked because it enabled her to show her contempt for the things other women valued.

She was much more extreme in her views on how to struggle against the existing order than her companions or her friend Tyurin were; she even asserted that all means could be used in the struggle for good, including murder. And yet deep down in her soul this revolutionary Katya Turchaninova was a very good, selfless woman, always quick to put the interests, enjoyment, and welfare of another before her own interests, enjoyment, and welfare, and always genuinely glad to have the chance to do someone a favor—a child, an old man, or an animal.

Turchaninova spent the summer with one of her friends, a country schoolteacher, in a district town in the Povolzh'e province. Tyurin was living with his father in the same district. The three of them, along with the local physician, often saw each other to exchange books, argue, and express their indignation. The Tyurin estate was right next to the Liventsov estate, where Petr Nikolaich had taken a job as manager. As soon as Petr Nikolaich arrived and started putting things in order, the young Tyurin took an interest in the peasants on the Liventsov estate, for he saw in them a kindred spirit, and he liked the stern measures they took to defend their rights. He often went to the village and talked with the peasants, promoting the theory of socialism in general and the nationalization of the land in particular.

When the murder of Petr Nikolaich took place and the trial was held, the group of revolutionaries in the district town had good reason to be outraged at the court and dared to say so. The things Tyurin discussed with the peasants when he would go to the village came out at the trial. They searched the Tyurin home and found several revolutionary brochures; the student was arrested and taken to Petersburg.

Turchaninova followed him and visited him at the prison. She was not allowed to see him on the usual visiting day but only when general gatherings were held, so that she and Tyurin could only see each other through two sets of iron bars. This visiting arrangement made her indignation run deeper still. And her talk with the handsome gendarme officer, who was obviously ready to make allowances if she should accept his propositions, drove her to the extreme limits of indignation. It drove her to the ultimate level of outrage against all authorities. She went to complain to the chief of police. He told her the same thing the gendarme did, that there was nothing they could do and that the matter was at the minister's disposition. She submitted a report to the minister's office asking for an appointment; she was refused. Then she decided to take more desperate measures: she bought a revolver.

XXII

The minister was taking appointments at his usual hour. He passed over three petitioners, received a governor, and then came to the beautiful, dark-eyed young woman dressed in black, standing there with a piece of paper in her left hand. An amorous, lustful flame lit up in the minister's eyes at the sight of the beautiful petitioner, but, mindful of his position, he assumed a serious expression.

"What can I do for you?" he asked as he approached her.

Without answering, she quickly pulled the hand holding the revolver out from under her cape, aimed at the minister's chest, fired, and missed.

The minister tried to grab her hand, but she jerked back and fired again. The minister turned to run. She was seized. She was trembling and could not speak. All of a sudden she broke out laughing hysterically. The minister was not even wounded.

That was it for Turchaninova. She was held in jail to await her trial. As for the minister, he received congratulations and condolences from the most highly placed officials, even from the sovereign himself, and was appointed as the head of a commission for investigating the conspiracy which had resulted in this crime.

There was, of course, no conspiracy. Nonetheless, the ranks of the public and secret police diligently pursued the investigation of all leads on the nonexistent conspiracy and conscientiously earned their salaries. They got up early in the morning, before daylight, and conducted search after search. They registered papers and books, read diaries and personal letters, and wrote down excerpts on excellent paper in excellent handwriting. They interrogated Turchaninova and repeatedly confronted her with the evidence, hoping to get the names of her accomplices from her.

The minister was a good man at heart and felt very sorry for this healthy, beautiful Cossack, but he told himself that on his shoulders lay the heavy civil responsibilities which he would fulfill, no matter how difficult it was for him. And when an old friend, a chamberlain who knew the Tyurins, saw him at a royal ball and asked about Tyurin and Turchaninova, the minister shrugged his shoulders, wrinkling the red ribbon on his white waistcoat, and said, "Je ne demanderais pas mieux que de lâcher cette pauvre fillette, mais vous savez—le devoir."*

In the meantime Turchaninova was being held while awaiting trial. Sometimes she quietly communicated with her comrades by tapping on the walls or read books that they gave to her; sometimes, however, she would suddenly fall into despair, scream and laugh, and wildly beat on the walls.

XXIII

One day, as she was returning home from picking up her pension at the treasury office, Mariya Semenovna ran into a schoolteacher she knew.

"Well, Mariya Semenovna, did you get your money?" he shouted from the other side of the street.

"I got it," Mariya Semenovna answered. "Only to pay some debts."

"Well, with your debts, you could pay them all and still have

*"There is nothing I would rather do than release the poor girl, but you understand —duty."

a lot of money left over," the teacher replied, and, saying good-bye, he walked on.

"Good-bye," said Mariya Semenovna; as she was watching the teacher walk off, she bumped into a tall man with very long arms and a stern face.

When she got to her house, she was surprised to see the same long-armed man again. After he watched her enter the house, he stood for a moment and then turned around and left.

At first Mariya Semenovna grew frightened, and then she felt sad. But she began to feel good again when she went into the house and handed out the presents she had bought for the old man and her scrofulous little nephew Fedya; she petted the dog Trezorka, who was yelping with joy. After she gave the money to her father, she started on the work that was never at an end for her.

The man she had bumped into was Stepan.

Stepan did not go to the city after he left the inn where he killed the innkeeper. Surprising as it may seem, he not only found the memory of the innkeeper's murder pleasant, but he recalled it several times a day. He liked the thought that he could do it so cleanly and cleverly, that no one would find out about it or even prevent him from doing it to someone else. As he sat down in a tavern for some tea and vodka, he would look at the people sitting all around him and think of how he could murder them.

He stopped in to spend the night with a man he knew, a drayman. The drayman was not home. Stepan said he would wait and sat down to chat with the man's wife. Then, as she turned to go to the stove, the thought entered his head that he might murder her. It surprised him; he gave his head a shake and then took a knife from his boot, pulled her down, and slit her throat. The children started to cry out; he killed them and left without spending the night in town. In a village outside of town he went to a tavern and there had a good sleep.

The next day he went back to the district town and heard Mariya Semenovna's conversation with the schoolteacher on the street. The look on her face frightened him, but he decided to break into her house anyway and take the money she had picked up. That night he broke the lock and went inside. The married, younger daughter was the first to see him. Stepan immediately stabbed her. The son-in-law woke up and struggled with him. He grabbed Stepan by the throat and fought with him for a long time, but Stepan was stronger. After he finished off the son-in-law, Stepan, alarmed and excited from the fight, slipped behind a partition. There Mariya Semenovna was lying in bed. She got up and stared at him with frightened but gentle eyes; she crossed herself. Once again the look on her face frightened Stepan. He lowered his eyes.

"Where's the money?" he asked without raising his eyes.

She said nothing.

"Where's the money?" he demanded, showing her the knife.

"Why are you doing this? Is it really necessary?" she said.

"It is."

Stepan went up to her, ready to grab her hands so she would not resist him; she neither raised her hands nor fought back but simply clasped them to her breast, sighed deeply, and said, "Oh, this is a great sin! Why are you doing this? Take pity on yourself. You are destroying other souls, and worse, your own . . . oh!" She uttered a scream.

Stepan could no longer bear the sound of her voice or the look on her face and cut her throat. "You think I'm going to argue with you?" She fell to the pillow and began to gasp as her blood flowed over the pillow. He turned away and walked around the room picking up things. Once he had collected what he wanted, Stepan lit a cigarette, sat down for a moment, straightened up his clothes, and left. He thought he would get away with this murder, just like the others; but before he could reach shelter for the night, he suddenly felt so weary that he could not move a limb. He lay down in a ditch and stayed there for the rest of the night, all the next day, and the following night.

Part Two

I

AS HE LAY IN THE DITCH, Stepan continually saw Mariya Semenovna's thin, gentle, frightened face before him, continually heard the sound of her voice. "Is this really necessary?" that peculiar, lisping, compassionate voice had said. Again and again Stepan relived what he had done to her. He grew terrified and closed his eyes and shook his hairy head to drive these thoughts and memories out of it. For a minute he would free himself of these memories, but in their place there appeared first a certain dark figure and then still other dark figures with red eyes. They made faces at him and said, "As you put an end to her life, so your life will be ended, for we shall give you no peace." And he opened his eyes and again saw her and heard her voice; he took pity on her and felt depraved and terrified. Again he closed his eyes and again—the dark figures.

Toward the evening of the following day he got up and went to a drinking house. He made his way there with difficulty; he started drinking. But no matter how much he drank, inebriation would not overtake him. He sat at the table without saying a word and drank glass after glass.

The town policeman came in.

"Who might you be?" the policeman asked.

"I'm the one who cut everyone's throat at the Dobrotvorov place the other day."

He was manacled, and after spending a day at police headquarters, was sent to the capital city of the province. The prison warden recognized him as a hoodlum who had once been a prisoner there and who was now a hardened criminal; he gave him a stern reception.

"I'll have none of your tricks, do you hear?" the warden said in a hoarse voice, wrinkling his brow and thrusting his lower jaw forward. "If you make one move, I'll have you flogged to death. You can't escape me."

"Why should I escape?" Stepan answered, lowering his eyes. "I turned myself in."

"Don't talk back to me. And when your superior speaks to you, look him in the eye," the warden shouted and hit Stepan in the jaw with his fist.

At that moment Stepan once again saw her before him and heard the sound of her voice. He did not hear what the warden was saying.

"Wha—?" he asked, collecting himself when he received the blow to his face.

"Oh, get out of here. There's nothing more to say."

After talking with other prisoners, the warden expected violence from Stepan or an attempt to escape. But there was nothing of the kind. Either the prison guard or the warden himself would peer through the small hole in his cell door to find Stepan sitting on the sack stuffed with straw with his head resting on his hands, whispering something to himself over and over. He was also unlike any other prisoner when the investigator interrogated him. He was absentminded and did not listen to the questions. When he did respond to them, he was so truthful that the investigator, who was used to dealing with cunning and evasiveness among accused prisoners, here felt the way you feel when you come to the top of a stairway in the dark and raise your foot to the next step only to find that there is none. With a wrinkled brow and his eyes focused on one spot, Stepan told all about the murders he had committed in a very simple, businesslike tone, trying to recall every detail.

"He came out," Stepan related his first murder, "in his

bare feet and stood in the doorway; then I let him have it. He began to gasp, and then I went straight for the woman. . . ." And so on.

When the public prosecutor was making his rounds through the prison cells, he asked Stepan whether he had any complaints or needed anything. Stepan replied that he needed nothing and that he was being treated well. The prosecutor walked a few steps down the stinking corridor and then stopped and asked the warden, who was accompanying him, how this prisoner was behaving himself.

"I'm amazed at him," the warden answered, pleased that Stepan had spoken well of the way he was being treated. "This is his second month with us, and his behavior has been exemplary. I'm only afraid that he may be planning something. He's a daring man of exceptional strength."

II

Throughout his first month in prison Stepan was continually tormented by the same thing: he saw the gray walls of his cell and heard the sounds of the jail—the rumbling from the general cell block beneath him, the guard's footsteps in the corridor, the ticking of his watch—and along with all that he saw her, with the gentle look on her face that overcame him from the moment he ran into her on the street and the thin, wrinkled throat he had cut. And he heard her tender, compassionate voice whispering, *"You are destroying other souls, as well as your own. Is this really necessary?"* Then her voice would grow silent and the three dark figures would appear. It did not matter whether his eyes were open or closed; they were there. He could see them more clearly with his eyes closed. When he opened his eyes, they would blend in with the door and the walls and fade a little. But then they appeared again and came toward him from three different sides, making faces at him and repeating the same thing over and over: end it all, end it all. He could make a noose or set a fire. At that point Stepan would be seized with trembling and began reciting what prayers he knew: the Hail Mary and the Our Father, and at first it seemed to help.

As he recited the prayers, he began to think back on his life: he remembered his mother and father, his dog Volchka, his grandfather at the stove, the benches on which he fidgeted with other children at school, the girls and their songs. Then he remembered his horses, how they were stolen, how the thief was caught, and how he beat him to death with a stone. He recalled his first time in jail and how he got out; he recalled the fat innkeeper, the drayman's wife and children, and then he remembered her. He started to feel hot and took off his coat; he jumped up from his plank bed and, like an animal in a cage, began pacing back and forth in the narrow cell with rapid steps, quickly turning at the damp, sweaty walls.

One long autumn evening, when the wind was whistling and buzzing in the flues, he sat down on his bed after pacing about his cell and felt that he could struggle no more, that the dark figures had overpowered him, and he surrendered to them. He stared at the vents in the heating stove for a long time. If he were to bind himself with thin bands or strips of canvas, then he would not slip off. But it had to be done properly. He started working on it, and in two days he had prepared some strips of canvas made from the sack of straw on which he slept (whenever the guard came in, he would cover the bed with his coat). He tied the strips together in knots and doubled them up so they would hold his weight without breaking. He was no longer tormented, as he was making all these preparations.

When everything was ready, he made the noose, put it around his neck, climbed onto the bed, and hanged himself. But just when his tongue started to stick out, the rope broke and he fell. Hearing the noise, the guard came in. He called a doctor's assistant and had Stepan taken to the infirmary. By the next day he had completely recovered; they took him and put him not in an isolated cell but in the general cell block.

He lived with twenty men in the general cell block, but it was as if he lived alone; he saw no one, spoke to no one, and continued in his torment. It was especially hard for him when everyone was sleeping, for he saw her as before and heard her voice, and then the dark figures with their terrible eyes would appear again and taunt him.

Again, as before, he would recite the prayers, and as before, they did not help.

Once, when she appeared to him after he had recited the prayers, he began to pray to her, to her ghost, asking her to leave him in peace, to forgive him. And when he fell to the worn-out sack of straw as morning drew nigh, he went into a deep sleep, and she came to him in a dream, with her thin, wrinkled throat cut open.

"Please, won't you forgive me?"

She stared at him with a gentle look and said nothing.

"Will you forgive me?"

He asked her three times. But she still said nothing. And he awoke. From then on it was easier for him; suddenly he came to his senses, looked around, and for the first time he began to make friends and talk with his comrades in the cell block.

III

Vasily had fallen into a life of crime; he was arrested, sentenced to exile, and now occupied the same cell block Stepan was in. Chuev was there too, having also been sentenced to deportation. Vasily was forever singing a song in his beautiful voice or telling his comrades about his adventures. Chuev, however, either worked at sewing something, from an overcoat to underwear, or read the Gospel and the Psalter.

When Stepan asked him why he was being exiled, Chuev said he was being punished for his true faith in Christ, because the priests who led the soul astray were unable to hear those people who lived by the Gospel and revealed it. And when Stepan asked him what the law of the Gospel consisted of, Chuev explained that according to the law of the Gospel, we should not pray to artificial gods but should worship in spirit and in truth. And he told the story of how he found out about this true faith from the lame tailor when the land was being divided up.

"Yes, but what happens when we do evil?" Stepan asked.

"It is all written here."

And Chuev read to him:

When the Son of Man shall come in his glory, and all the holy angels with him, then shall he sit on the throne of his glory, and the peoples of all nations shall be gathered before him; and he shall separate one from the other, as a shepherd divides the sheep from the goats, and he shall place the sheep on his right and the goats on his left. Then the King shall say to those on his right, "Come, you who are blessed of my Father, inherit the kingdom prepared for you since the creation of the world: for I was hungry, and you gave me food; I was thirsty, and you gave me drink;

I was a stranger, and you took me in; I was naked, and you clothed me; I was sick, and you visited me; I was in prison, and you came to me." Then the righteous shall answer him, saying, "Lord, when did we see you hungry and feed you or thirsty and give you drink? When did we see you a stranger and take you in or naked and clothe you? When did we see you sick or in prison and come to you?" And the King shall answer them, saying, "Verily I say unto you, because you have done this for the least of my brothers, you have done it for me."

Then he shall say to those on his left, "Depart from me, you who are cursed, into the eternal fire prepared for the devil and his angels: for I was hungry, and you gave me nothing to eat; I was thirsty, and you gave me nothing to drink; I was a stranger, and you did not take me in; I was naked, and you did not clothe me, sick and in prison, and you did not visit me." Then they too shall answer him, saying, "Lord, when did we see you hungry or thirsty or a stranger or naked or sick or in prison and did not serve you?" Then he shall answer them, saying, "Verily I say unto you, because you failed to do this for the least of my brothers, you have failed to do it for me."

And these shall go to everlasting torment, and the righteous to eternal life. [Matthew 25 : 31–46]

Vasily had come to sit on the floor in front of Chuev and had listened to the reading; he nodded his handsome head in approval.

"It's true," he said decisively. "It says the damned will go to eternal torment for feeding no one and gorging themselves. They deserve it." Then, wanting to show off his reading ability, he added, "Here, let me have it; I'll read."

"And will there really be no forgiveness?" asked Stepan, who had quietly listened to the reading with his shaggy head bowed.

"Wait a minute and be quiet," Chuev said to Vasily, who was still going on about how the rich do not feed strangers or visit anyone in prison. "Wait a minute, will you?" Chuev repeated, thumbing through the Gospel. When he found what he was looking for, he smoothed out the page with his big, strong hand that had turned white in prison. He began:

And two criminals who were condemned to death were taken out with him. ["That is, with Christ," Chuev interjected.] And when they came to the place called Calvary, there they crucified him with the criminals, one on his right and one on his left.

And Jesus said, "Father, forgive them, for they know not what they do. . . ."

And the people stood and looked. And the officials who were there with them mocked him, saying, "He saved others; let him now save himself, if he is the Christ, the one God has chosen." The soldiers also abused him, coming up to him and offering him vinegar, saying, "If you are the King of the Jews, then save yourself." And there was an inscription written above him in Greek, Latin, and Hebrew: "This is the King of the Jews."

One of the criminals hanging there maligned him and said, "If you are the Christ, then save yourself and us." But the other one restrained him and said, "Have you no fear of God, when you yourself are con-demned to the same fate? We have been justly condemned and have gotten what we deserve. But he has done nothing wrong." And he said to Jesus, "Remember me, Lord, when you enter your kingdom." And Jesus said to him, "Verily I say unto you, today you shall be with me in paradise." [Luke 23 : 32–43]

Stepan said nothing and sat immersed in thought; he appeared to be listening, but he heard nothing after Chuev had stopped reading.

"That's where true faith lies," he thought. "Only those shall be saved who give food and drink to the poor and who visit prisoners, while those who do not do this will go to hell. And even the thief who did not repent until he was on the cross went to paradise."

He saw no contradiction in this; on the contrary, one text supported the other. The fact that those who are kind will enter paradise and those who are not will go to hell meant that all must be kind; and the fact that Christ did forgive meant that Christ too was kind. All this was completely new to Stepan; the thing that surprised him was that it had been hidden from him until then. He spent all his free time with Chuev, asking him questions and listening to him. And as he listened, he understood. It was revealed to him that the general meaning of all the teachings was that all people are brothers, that we should love one another and have compassion for each other, and then all will be well. And when he listened, he comprehended everything which confirmed the general meaning of this teaching, as if it were something he had known but had forgotten; and he disregarded everything which did not confirm it, attributing that to his lack of understanding.

From that time on Stepan became a different man.

IV

Stepan Pelageyushkin had been a humble man before then, but lately the change which had taken place in him was amazing the warden, the guards, and his comrades. Without being ordered or waiting his turn, he performed the most difficult tasks, including cleaning the latrine. Yet despite his humility, his fellow prisoners respected and feared him, knowing his great strength and tenacity, especially after the incident with the two vagrants who jumped him; he defended himself from both of them and broke the arm of one of them. These tramps lured a young, well-to-do prisoner into a card game and took everything he had. Stepan stepped in to help him get back the money they had won. The tramps called him names and then started hitting him, but he overpowered both of them. When the warden asked what the argument was about, the tramps claimed that Pelageyushkin just came up and started beating them. Stepan did not deny it and calmly accepted his punishment, which was three days in the detention cell and transfer to solitary confinement.

Solitary confinement was hard for him in that it isolated him from Chuev and the Gospel; he was also afraid that the visions of her and the dark figures would return. But there were no visions. His whole soul was filled with a new and joyous substance. He would have been happy about his solitude, if he had been able to read and if he had had a Gospel. And they would have given him a Gospel, but he could not read.

As a schoolboy he had begun to study grammar long ago: A, B, C, but he could not get beyond the alphabet from lack of understanding; he was completely unable to spell and so remained illiterate. But now he decided to study hard and asked the guard for a Gospel. The guard brought him one, and he started to work. He recognized the letters but could not put anything together. No matter how much he struggled to understand the words formed by the letters, he could come up with nothing. Instead of sleeping at night, he thought. In his depression, he refused to eat; such a worm had fallen upon his heart that he could not get rid of it.

"What's the matter, aren't you getting anywhere?" the guard asked him one day.

"No."

"You know the Lord's Prayer, don't you?"

"Yes, I know it."

"Well, here, read it. Here it is," the guard showed him the Lord's Prayer in the Gospel.

Stepan began reading the Lord's Prayer, correlating the familiar letters with the familiar sounds. And suddenly the secret of how to put the letters together was revealed to him, and he started to read. It was a profound joy. He continued to read from that time on, gradually deciphering the meaning from the words which were arranged in such a difficult manner, until he derived an even greater significance from them.

Now his solitude no longer weighed upon Stepan but gladdened him. He was completely absorbed in his business and was not very happy when he was transferred back to the general cell block in order to make room for political prisoners.

V

It was no longer Chuev, but Stepan who was frequently reading the Gospel in the cell block; while some of the convicts sang bawdy songs, others listened to his readings and to the discussions of what was read. Two of the prisoners always listened to him quietly and attentively: a murderer and executioner named Makhorkin, and Vasily, who had been arrested for stealing and was awaiting trial in this very jail. Twice before during his confinement in prison, Makhorkin had performed his duty as executioner, since they could find no one else who was willing to carry out the judges' sentence. Now the peasants who killed Petr Nikolaich had been tried by a military court, and two of them had been sentenced to death by hanging.

Makhorkin was needed in Penza to carry out the duty he performed. Formerly, under such circumstances he would have immediately written a letter to the governor—he was quite literate —explaining that he had been commissioned to perform his duty in Penza and asking that the head of the province allot him the daily eating allowance which was his due. Now, however, much to the surprise of the head of the prison, he declared that he would not do it and would no longer perform his duty as executioner.

"Have you forgotten the lash?" the head of the prison shouted.

"Well, the lash is only the lash, but killing is unlawful."

"I suppose you got that from Pelageyushkin. There is a prophet in the prison, but you just wait."

VI

Meanwhile Makhin, the gymnasium student who taught his friend how to forge a coupon, graduated from the gymnasium and then from the university law school. Thanks to his success with women, particularly with the former lover of an old man who was a friend of the minister, he was appointed as court investigator while he was still quite young. He was a dishonest man when it came to paying his debts; he was a gambler and a seducer of women. But he was also a clever, resourceful man with a good memory and knew how to conduct his affairs.

He was the court investigator in the district where Stepan Pelageyushkin was tried. At the very first interrogation Stepan surprised Makhin with his simple, truthful, and calm answers to the questions. Makhin instinctively felt that this man, who stood before him with his head shaved and his hands in shackles, who had been brought in by two soldiers that now guarded him, and who would be taken away under lock and key—he felt that this man was totally free and on a moral level that was inaccessibly higher than his own. And so as he interrogated him Makhin was constantly reassuring himself and urging himself on, so that he would not become embarrassed and confused. He was particularly struck by the way Stepan spoke of his deeds as if they belonged to some remote past, committed not by him but by some other man.

"And did you have no pity on them?" Makhin asked.

"I felt no pity. I didn't understand then."

"And now?"

Stepan smiled in a sad way.

"Now a flame burns within me, in spite of what I have done."

"And where does it come from?"

"From the realization that all people are brothers."

"What do you mean? Am I your brother?"

"You are indeed."

"How is it that I am your brother, and yet I send you to hard labor?"

"It is from a lack of understanding."

"What exactly do I fail to understand?"

"If you judge, you do not understand."

"Well, let's continue. Where did you go next . . . ?"

The thing which struck Makhin most of all was what he found out from the warden about Pelageyushkin's influence on the executioner Makhorkin, who had refused to perform his duty at the risk of being punished.

VII

In the Eropkin home there lived two daughters who would make wealthy brides, and Makhin was courting both of them. The evening following the interrogation—after the three of them sang some romantic songs, in which he beautifully displayed his musical

talents, taking the second part and accompanying the girls—
Makhin told the story of the strange criminal who had converted
the executioner, and told it with complete indifference, truthfully
and in detail (he had an excellent memory). The reason why
Makhin had such a good memory and could relate everything in
detail was that he was always totally indifferent toward the people
he dealt with. He did not enter—indeed, he did not know how
to enter—into emotional relationships with people and therefore
could recall so well everything that happened to them, everything
they did and said.

Yet he took an interest in Pelageyushkin. He did not probe
Stepan's soul, but he could not help posing the question of what
lay in the man's soul. He found no answers, but since he was
convinced it was something interesting, he told the whole story
that evening: the corruption of the executioner, the warden's
account of how strangely Pelageyushkin behaved, how he read the
Gospel, and what a powerful influence he had on the other prisoners.

Everyone was fascinated by Makhin's tale, especially young
Liza Eropkina, an eighteen-year-old girl who had just graduated
from the institute and had just become aware of the darkness and
narrowness of the phony environment in which she had grown up;
it was as though she had emerged from the deep to breathe the
fresh air of life. She started asking Makhin about the details of why
such a change had taken place in Pelageyushkin. Makhin explained what Stepan had told him about his last murder—how the
gentleness, humility, and fearlessness of that good woman, even
in the face of death, had overwhelmed him and opened his eyes,
and how he finally came to read the Gospel.

Liza Eropkina could not go to sleep for a long time that night.
For several months now there had been a struggle within her

between the worldly life into which her sister had been drawn and her passion for Makhin, which was shaped by a desire to reform him. And now the latter prevailed. She had heard about the murdered woman before. But now, after listening to Makhin's story of what Pelageyushkin had said, she had learned all the details of Mariya Semenovna's terrible death and was quite struck by what she had learned. Liza burned with a passion to be like Mariya Semenovna. She was rich and was afraid Makhin was courting her because of her money. And she decided to give away her property and told Makhin about her decision.

Makhin was glad to have the opportunity to demonstrate his unselfishness and told Liza that he did not love her because of her money, that he thought this was a magnanimous decision, and that it touched him deeply. In the meantime, a battle broke out between Liza and her mother (the property had belonged to her father); her mother refused to allow her to give away the property. Makhin helped Liza. And the more he acted in such a manner, the more he understood that peace of spiritual aspiration which he saw in Liza and which, until that time, had been utterly foreign to him.

VIII

All was quiet in the cell block. Stepan was lying on his plank bed and was not asleep yet. Vasily went up to him, grabbed him by the foot, and signaled for him to get up and go with him. Stepan slipped down from the bunk and went with Vasily.

"Listen, brother," said Vasily. "I wonder if you'd be kind enough to do me a favor."

"What favor?"

"I'm planning to escape."

And Vasily revealed to Stepan that he had everything ready for an escape.

"Tomorrow I'm going to rile them up," he pointed to the prisoners who were lying in their beds. "They'll inform on me. I'll be taken upstairs, and I know what to do after that. I just want you to pull out the lock to the morgue."

"That can be done. Where will you go?"

"Wherever my eyes lead me. Is it true that very few people are bad?"

"It is true, brother, but it is not for us to judge them."

"Well, I suppose I may be a murderer at heart. I've never killed anyone, though. As for stealing, what's wrong with that? Isn't it true that people steal from their brothers?"

"That's their affair. They will answer for it."

"What are they going to do, gnash their teeth? Look, I once robbed a church. Did that hurt anyone? I'm not planning to knock off some little shop; I'm going to hit a treasury office or something and give the money away. Give it to good people."

At that moment one of the convicts got up from his bed and started listening. Stepan and Vasily split up.

The next day Vasily did what he had planned to do. He began complaining that the bread was damp, and he incited the prisoners to call for the warden and state their complaint. The warden came in, swore at them, and found out that Vasily had been the instigator of the affair; he had Vasily taken to solitary confinement on the upper level. That was all Vasily needed.

IX

Vasily was familiar with the upper-level cell where they took him. He knew the floor plan, and as soon as he was in there, he began tearing out the floor. When he could climb through, he tore out the ceiling below and jumped down to the lower level, into the morgue. There was one dead man lying in the morgue that day. Sacks for straw mattresses were also piled in there. Vasily knew this and was counting on it. The lock to the morgue had been pulled out and slipped back into place. Vasily went out the door and down to a latrine that was under construction at the end of the corridor. In the latrine there was a shaft that went from the second floor on down to the basement.

After fumbling at the door, Vasily went back into the morgue and took the sheet off the dead man, who was cold as ice (he had touched his hand when he pulled the sheet off). Then he took the sacks, tied them together to form a rope, and carried the rope of sacks down to the latrine; there he tied the rope to a beam and climbed down the shaft to the basement. The rope did not reach the floor. Perhaps it was too short—he did not know, but there was nothing he could do about it; so after hanging there a moment, he let go. He hurt his legs, but he could still walk.

There were two windows in the basement. He could climb through one of them, but they were covered with iron gratings. He would have to break through. But how? Vasily started rummaging around. He found two boards lying in the basement. He picked up the one with a sharp end and started chipping away at the brickwork that was holding one of the gratings. He worked at it for a long time. The roosters were already crowing for the second time, and still the grating held. Finally, one side came loose. Vasily shoved the board under it and pried; the grating came undone, but a brick fell out and came down with a crash. The sentries could have heard it. Vasily froze. All was quiet. He climbed through the window. He was out.

Now he had to get over the wall. There was an annex in the corner of the prison yard. He would have to climb up on top of it and go over the wall from there. He needed a board; he could not climb up without it. Vasily slipped back through the window. He climbed out again with the board and stood still, listening to see if he could tell where the sentry was. He figured the sentry was walking along the other side of the prison yard. Vasily went up to the annex, put the board in place, and started to climb up. The board slipped and fell. Vasily was in his stocking feet. He pulled his socks off so he could hang on with his feet; he put the board back in place, jumped up on it, and grabbed hold of the gutter with one hand.

"God, don't break off, hold me."

He gripped the gutter and got his knee up on the roof. The sentry was coming. Vasily lay still. The sentry did not see him and went away. Vasily jumped up. The iron creaked under his feet. One more step, then two, and there was the wall. It was easy to reach the top of the wall with his hand. He stretched out one hand, then the other, and he was on the wall. Just don't get hurt jumping off. Vasily climbed over and was hanging by his hands; he stretched himself out and let go, first one hand and then the other.

"Lord, thank you!"

On the ground. And the ground was soft. His legs were fine, and he ran.

In an outlying town a girl named Malan'ya unlocked her door

for him, and he snuggled under a warm blanket that was quilted from bits and pieces of cloth and saturated with the smell of sweat.

X

Tall, beautiful, forever calm, childless, and plump as a dry cow, Petr Nikolaich's wife was watching through the window when her husband was killed and dragged off to the fields somewhere. While she looked upon the slaughter, the feeling of horror that went through Natal'ya Ivanovna (as Petr Nikolaich's widow was called) was so strong that it smothered all other feelings in her, as one might expect. After the crowd had disappeared behind the garden fence and the sounds of their voices had died away, the barefoot servant girl Malan'ya came running, wide-eyed, with the news that Petr Nikolaich had been killed and thrown into a ravine, as if it were something to rejoice about. At that point Natal'ya Ivanovna's initial sensation of horror began to give way to another sensation: it was a feeling of joy over her liberation from the despot in the dark glasses that hid the eyes which enslaved her for nineteen years. She was terrified of this feeling and would not admit it to herself, much less tell anyone else about it.

While the hairy, yellow, disfigured body was being washed, dressed, and laid into the coffin, she was horrified and cried with heavy sobs. The investigator came to handle this important matter personally and called her to his quarters to question her as a witness; there she saw two peasants in chains who had been iden-tified as the main guilty parties. One of them was an old man with a long, white, curly beard and a handsome face, calm yet stern; the other was of gypsy stock, rather young, with flashing dark eyes and curly, disheveled hair. She told the investigator what she knew and identified these men as the ones who were the first to grab Petr Nikolaich by the arms. Despite the fact that the gypsy and the peasant alike, their eyes flashing and shifting under their trembling brows, shouted reproachfully, "It's a mistake, madame! We shall die!"—despite their outcries, she took no pity on them. Quite the contrary, during the investigation a feeling of hostility and the desire to avenge the murder of her husband rose up within her.

When the matter was taken to the military court a month later, eight men were sentenced to hard labor and two—the old man with the white beard and the dark-complected little gypsy, as everyone called him—were sentenced to be hanged. An unpleasant sensation went through Natal'ya Ivanovna. But this unpleasant doubt, influenced by the solemnity of the court, soon passed. If the higher authorities deemed it necessary, then it must be good.

The execution was to take place in the village. When Malan'ya returned from her Sunday dinner wearing a new dress and new shoes, she announced to the lady that the gallows were being built, that an executioner was expected to arrive from Moscow by the middle of the week, and that the prisoners' families were wailing incessantly and could be heard all over the village.

Natal'ya Ivanovna did not leave the house, so that she would not see the gallows or the people. She wanted only one thing: that what must be done be over as soon as possible. She was thinking only of herself, and not of the condemned men or their families.

XI

On Tuesday the district police officer, who was a friend of hers, came to visit Natal'ya Ivanovna. She treated him to vodka and some salted mushrooms she had made. After the vodka and the snack, the police officer informed her that the execution planned for the following day would not take place.

"What? Why not?"

"It's a surprising story. No executioner can be found. My son told me that the one in Moscow started reading the Gospel and says he will not kill anymore. He was sentenced to hard labor for murder, and now, suddenly, he cannot kill because it's against the law. They told him they would beat him with a whip. 'Whip me,' he says, 'I cannot do it.' "

Natal'ya Ivanovna suddenly flushed and even broke out in a sweat at the thought of it.

"And is there no way to pardon them now?"

"How can they be pardoned when the court has pronounced sentence? Only the tsar can pardon them."

"And how can the tsar find out about it?"

"He has the right to grant a pardon on the basis of an appeal."

"But they are being executed because of me," said the foolish Natal'ya Ivanovna. "And I forgive them."

The police officer smiled.

"Well, then, intercede for them."

"Can I?"

"Sure you can."

"Is there still time?"

"You can send a telegram."

"To the tsar?"

"The tsar can get telegrams too."

Natal'ya Ivanovna's soul did a sudden turnabout when she heard that the executioner had refused and was even prepared to suffer rather than kill; and the feeling of compassion and horror which had surfaced a few times now burst forth and seized her.

"My dear Filipp Vasil'evich, send the telegram for me. I want to appeal to the tsar for a pardon."

The police officer shook his head.

"Even though we may be reprimanded for it?"

"I'm the one who's responsible. I won't say anything about you."

And the policeman thought, "What a kind woman, a good woman. If I had such a woman, it would be paradise, and not the way it is now."

The police officer sent the telegram to the tsar: "To His Imperial Majesty the Tsar, Emperor. Your Imperial Majesty's loyal subject, the widow of the collegiate assessor Petr Nikolaevich Sventitsky, who was murdered by peasants, wishes to follow in Your Imperial Majesty's holy footsteps [the policeman was especially pleased with the way he composed this portion of the telegram] and beseeches You to pardon the peasants sentenced to death in this such-and-such a province, district, jurisdiction, village."

The police officer sent the telegram himself, and in her soul Natal'ya Ivanovna felt joyful and good. She believed that if she, the widow of the murdered man, should forgive and ask for a pardon, then the tsar could not help but grant the pardon.

XII

Liza Eropkina was living in a state of continuous rapture. The farther she walked down the path of Christian life that had been revealed to her, the more certain she became that this was the path of truth, and the more profound was the joy she felt in her soul.

She now had two immediate goals. The first was to convert Makhin, or rather, as she put it, to turn him back to himself, to his own good, beautiful nature. She loved him, and in the light of her love the divinity of his soul was revealed to her and to people in general; and in the life he undertook to live for all people she saw the genuine goodness, tenderness, and eminence that was his alone.

Her second goal was to get rid of her wealth. She wanted to free herself from property in order to test Makhin, as well as for her own sake, for the sake of her soul—in accordance with the words of the Gospel, she wanted to do this. When she first started giving it away, her father stopped her; and even more problematic than her father was the crowd of supplicants who assailed her both in person and through the mail. Then she decided to go to a monk who was known for his holy life and ask him to take her money and use it as he saw fit. When her father found out about it, he became very angry. In a heated discussion he called her a madwoman, a psychopath, and said he would take measures to protect her from herself, since she had gone mad.

She took on her father's angry, exasperated tone. Unable to control herself, she burst into tears of rage and accused her father of barbarity, calling him a despotic and even a mercenary man.

She asked her father's forgiveness, and he said he was not

angry anymore, but she saw that he had been offended and in his heart did not forgive her. She did not want to tell Makhin about this. Her sister, who was jealous of her over Makhin, shunned her completely. Liza did not share her feelings or confess them to anyone.

"One must confess to God," she told herself. Since it was Lent, she decided to fast and at confession tell everything to the father confessor and ask his advice on what she should do next.

Not far from the city was a monastery, where there lived a monk who was famous for the life he led, for the sermons, the prophecies, and the healings attributed to him.

The monk received a letter from the elder Eropkin, letting him know that Liza was coming, warning him about her abnormal, excited condition, and expressing the certainty that the monk would lead her back to the true path—to the golden mean of the good Christian life—without disturbing the status quo.

Weary from receiving visitors, the monk saw Liza and suggested moderation, submission to the status quo, and obedience to her parents. Liza grew silent, turned red, and broke out in a sweat; but when the monk had finished, she spoke—timidly at first, with tears in her eyes—of what Christ had said: "Forsake your mother and father and follow me."* Then, as she became more and more inspired, she expressed all her views on how she understood Christianity. At first the monk smiled slightly and responded with the usual precepts, but then he fell silent and sighed now and then, repeating, "Oh, Lord!"

"Very well, come tomorrow for confession," he said, and he blessed her with his wrinkled hand.

The next day he heard her confession; he granted her absolu-

---

*Compare this to Matthew 10 : 37 and Luke 14 : 26.

tion, and without continuing their conversation from the previous day, he briefly refused to take upon himself the disposal of her property.

The monk was amazed at this young woman's purity, passion, and complete devotion to the will of God. For a long time he had wanted to renounce the world, but the monastery demanded that he be active in the world. This activity provided the monastery with means of support. So he consented, although he had a vague notion of all the falsehood of his position. He was regarded as a holy man, a worker of miracles, yet he was a weak man tempted by success. As the soul of this young woman was revealed to him, so too was his own soul. And he saw how far he was from what he longed to be and what it was that held sway over his heart.

Soon after his meeting with Liza, he locked himself into seclusion; it was not until three weeks later that he came out to go to the church, where he conducted the service and then gave a sermon in which he confessed himself and exposed the world for its sin, calling upon it to repent.

Every two weeks he gave a sermon. And the people gathered at these sermons in ever-increasing numbers. And his renown as a preacher spread far and wide. There was something special, bold, and sincere in his sermons. And because of this, he had such a powerful effect on people.

XIII

Meanwhile Vasily did what he set out to do. After leaving his comrades, he made his way one night to the home of a rich man named Krasnopuzov. He knew what a miser and debauchee the man was and got into his bureau and took some thirty thousand rubles. Then Vasily did what he had planned to do; he even stopped drinking. He gave money to destitute girls of marriageable age. He helped them to get married, paid their debts, and then went into hiding. The one worry he had was to do a good job of giving away the money. He even gave some to the police, so they would stop looking for him.

His heart was filled with joy. And when he was finally apprehended again, he laughed at his trial and boasted that the potbellied rich man used the money badly, that he did not even know how to count it, "while I put it to use and helped good people with it."

His defense was so cheerful, so good-natured, that the jurors almost acquitted him. He was sentenced to exile.

He thanked the court and had told them beforehand that he would accept exile.

XIV

Sventitskaya's telegram to the tsar produced no results. At first the petitions committee decided not to report it to the tsar; but when the Sventitsky case came up in conversation at a luncheon with His Majesty, the chairman of the committee mentioned the telegram from the wife of the murdered man.

"C'est très gentil de sa part,"* said one of the ladies of the royal family.

His Majesty heaved a sigh, shrugged the epaulets on his shoulders, and said, "It's the law." Then he held up his glass, into which the lackey in attendance poured sparkling Moselle. Everyone took

*"It is very kind of her."

on a look of astonishment at the wisdom of the words spoken by
His Majesty. Nothing more was said about the telegram. And the
two peasants—the old one and the young one—were hanged with
the help of a Tartar executioner ordered from Kazan, a man who
was a ruthless murderer and a sodomite.

The old man's wife wanted to dress her husband's body in a
white shirt, white leggings, and new boots, but she was not allowed
to do so, and both men were buried in a common pit behind the
churchyard fence.

"Princess Sof'ya Vladimirovna told me that he is an amazing
preacher," His Majesty's mother the Dowager Empress said to her
son. "Faites le venir. Il peut prêcher à la cathédrale."*

"No, we have a better one," His Majesty replied, and he
ordered the monk Isidor to be invited to preach.

The entire general staff attended the royal church. A new,
unusual preacher was going to be there.

A little old man, thin and gray, came out and looked at everyone. "In the name of the Father, the Son, and the Holy Spirit,"
he began.

At first it went well, but then it got worse. "Il devenait de plus
en plus aggressif,"† as the Dowager Empress put it. He railed
against everyone. He spoke on capital punishment. And he attributed the need for capital punishment to bad government. Is
it really possible to kill people in a Christian nation?

Everyone looked at each other; they were all concerned about
the impropriety and how distasteful it must be to His Majesty, but
no one said anything. When Isidor had said "Amen," the metro-

*"Invite him to come. He can preach at the cathedral."
†"He is becoming more and more aggressive."

politan went up to him and asked him to go with him.

After a talk with the metropolitan and the attorney-general, the little old man was immediately sent back to the monastery, not to his own but to the Suzdal' monastery, where Father Mikhail was the Father Superior and superintendent.

XV

Everyone adopted the attitude that there was nothing unpleasant about Isidor's sermon, and no one mentioned it. It seemed that even in the tsar no trace of the monk's words remained, but twice that day he recalled the execution of the peasants and the pardon Sventitskaya had requested in her telegram. There was a parade that afternoon, then a stroll, then the reception for the ministers, then dinner, then the theater that evening. As usual, the tsar fell asleep as soon as his head hit the pillow. That night he was awakened by a terrible dream: gallows were standing in a field with dead bodies swaying from them. The tongues of the dead men were hanging out, and they stretched out farther and farther. And someone cried, "This is your doing, your doing!" The tsar woke up in a sweat and started thinking. For the first time he started thinking about the responsibility that lay on his shoulders, and he recalled all the words the little old man had spoken. . . .

But it was only from a distance that he saw the human being in himself, and he could not separate the simple demands on him as a human being from the demands that laid claim to him from every quarter as the tsar. He did not have the strength to acknowledge that the demands on the human being were more binding than the demands on the tsar.

XVI

After serving a second term in prison, Proshka—that smart, proud, dandy of a fellow—left in a state of being utterly lost. When he was sober, he sat around and did nothing; no matter how much his father scolded him, he would eat his bread but would not work. Not only that, he would wait for the chance to steal something so he could go off to the tavern and get drunk. He would sit, hack, cough, and spit.

He went to a doctor, who listened to his chest and with a shake of the head said, "Brother, you need something you're not getting."

"Of course. That's what I always need."

"Drink milk and quit smoking."

"I don't feel like quitting right now; besides, I don't have a milk cow."

One night in the spring he could not get to sleep at all; he felt depressed and wanted to go out for a drink. There was nothing to keep him home. He put on his cap and went out. He walked until he came to where a priest lived. There was a harrow leaning against a fence outside the sexton's quarters. He lifted the harrow onto his back and started to take it to Petrovna at the tavern. "Perhaps she'll give me a little bottle." Just as he was about to leave, the sexton came out onto the porch. It was already quite light, and he saw that Proshka was carrying off the harrow.

"Hey, what do you think you're doing?"

Some people came out, grabbed Proshka, and put him in the cooler. The justice of the peace sentenced him to eleven months in prison.

It was autumn. Proshka was taken to the infirmary. He had a terrible cough that tore his whole chest apart. And he could not get warm. Those who were stronger were not shivering. But Proshka shivered day and night. The warden was economizing on firewood, and the infirmary did not get any heat until November. Proshka's body suffered terribly, but his soul suffered even more. He was disgusted with everything and he hated everyone: the sexton, the warden for not heating the infirmary, the guard, and the man on a neighboring cot with the swollen red lip. And he was starting to hate that new convict they had brought in.

The convict was Stepan. He was suffering from erysipelas on his head, and when they admitted him to the infirmary, they put him right next to Proshka. At first Proshka hated him, but then he came to love him so much that he lived only to talk with him. Only after a conversation with him did the torment in Proshka's heart subside.

Stepan always told everyone about his last murder and the effect it had on him.

"It does no good to scream and cry about it," he would say, "so pluck out what offends you. Not for my sake, as he says, but for your own."

"Well, everyone knows it is a terrible thing to waste a soul. I once set out to slaughter a ram, and I wasn't too happy about it. I've never ruined anyone, but for that the scoundrels have destroyed me. I've never hurt anyone. . . ."

"And that will be credited to your account."

"Where?"

"What do you mean 'where?' Don't you believe in God?"

"I've never seen Him; I don't believe, brother. I think you die —and the grass grows over you. That's all there is to it."

"How can you think that? I've destroyed so many people,

while she, that loving woman, only helped people. Do you really think that she and I will meet the same end? No, you just wait. . . ."

"So you think that when you die, your soul will continue?"

"Precisely. It is certain."

Proshka did not die easily; he was gasping for breath. But in his last hour, it suddenly became easier for him. He called out to Stepan.

"Farewell, brother. You can see that death has come for me. And what I had feared is now nothing. I only wish it would come quickly."

And Proshka died in the infirmary.

XVII

Meanwhile Evgeny Mikhailovich's affairs were getting worse and worse. The shop was mortgaged. Business was bad. Another shop had opened in the city, and his interest was due. He had to borrow more to pay the interest. He ended up with his shop and all his merchandise being put up for sale. Evgeny Mikhailovich and his wife rushed around far and near, but nowhere could they get the four hundred rubles they needed to save the business.

There had been one small hope with the merchant Krasnopuzov, whose mistress was a friend of Evgeny Mikhailovich's wife. Now, however, everyone in the city knew that a huge sum of money had been stolen from Krasnopuzov. It was said that he had lost half a million.

"And do you know who stole it?" Evgeny Mikhailovich's wife asked him. "Vasily, our old groundskeeper. They say that now he's blowing the money right and left and that he bribed the police."

"He was a wretch," said Evgeny Mikhailovich. "It was so easy for him to commit perjury back then. I never would have thought."

"They say he came by our place, through the courtyard. The cook said it was he. She says he helped fourteen poor young girls to get married."

"Well, they do make up stories, you know."

At that moment a strange elderly man in a tattered jacket came into the shop.

"What can we do for you?"

"A letter for you."

"From whom?"

"It's written there."

"Don't you require an answer? Wait a minute."

"It isn't necessary."

And having delivered the envelope, the strange man quickly left.

Evgeny Mikhailovich tore open the thick envelope and could not believe his eyes: hundred-ruble notes. Four of them. What is this? There was also a note to Evgeny Mikhailovich written in an illiterate hand: "As it is wrote in the Gospel, retern good fer evil. You did me a bad wrong over the koopon, I even hurt the pezent too, but I've took pity on you. So take these four Cathrins and rememer yer groundskeeper Vasily."

"No! It's amazing!" Evgeny Mikhailovich said to his wife, as well as to himself. And whenever he later recalled that moment or spoke of it to his wife, tears came to his eyes and his soul was filled with joy.

XVIII

Fourteen clergymen were being held in the Suzdal' prison, all of them mainly for deviation from orthodox beliefs; Isidor was among those sent there. Father Mikhail received him as ordered, and without speaking to him, had him placed in solitary confinement, like an important criminal. The third week of Isidor's confinement in the prison, Father Mikhail went to see those who were being held there. He stopped in to see Isidor and asked whether he needed anything.

"I need a great deal, but I cannot speak in front of people. Give me a chance to talk with you alone."

As they looked at each other, Father Mikhail realized that Isidor was not afraid of anything. He ordered Isidor to be brought to his quarters, and when they were alone, he said, "Well, speak."

Isidor fell to his knees.

"Brother!" cried Isidor. "What are you doing? Have pity on yourself. For there is no villain worse than you. You have broken with all that is holy. . . ."

A month later Mikhail submitted papers for the release not only of Isidor but of seven others as penitents and asked that he himself be allowed to retire to the monastery.

XIX

Ten years went by.

Mitya Smokovnikov graduated from a technical school and became an engineer with a good salary at the gold mine in Siberia. He had to travel throughout the region. His director suggested that he take along the convict Stepan Pelageyushkin.

"A convict? Isn't it dangerous?"

"There's no danger with him. He's a holy man. Ask anyone."

"So what was he convicted of?"

The director smiled.

"He murdered six people, but he's a holy man. I guarantee it."

And Mitya Smokovnikov took Stepan, a balding, thin, tanned man, and traveled with him.

Along the way Stepan cared for everyone wherever he went as if they were his own children; he cared for Smokovnikov and told him his entire story while they were on the road. And he told him how, why, and what he now lived for.

An astonishing thing happened. Mitya Smokovnikov—who up until now had lived only for food, drink, cards, wine, and women —began to reflect on his life for the first time. And these thoughts did not leave him but more and more turned his soul upside down. He was offered a position that would bring him tremendous advantages. He turned it down; he decided to take what he had and buy some property, get married, and serve the people as best he knew how.

XX

And he did so. But first he went to his father; he had been on bad terms with him ever since his father had left home to take on a new family. Now, however, he decided to reconcile with his father. And he did so. At first his father was taken aback and made fun of him. But then he stopped abusing him, for he recalled the many, many times when he had been guilty before his son.

1880–1904